THE SECRET OF GLENDUNNY

❖

Book 2

The Searchers

OTHER BOOKS BY KATHRYN LASKY

The Secret of Glendunny: The Haunting

Faceless

She Caught the Light

Night Witches

Tangled in Time: The Portal

Tangled in Time: The Burning Queen

Guardians of Ga'Hoole

Wolves of the Beyond

Horses of the Dawn

Bears of the Ice

Daughters of the Sea

The Royal Diaries: Elizabeth I

The Royal Diaries: Mary, Queen of Scots

The Deadlies

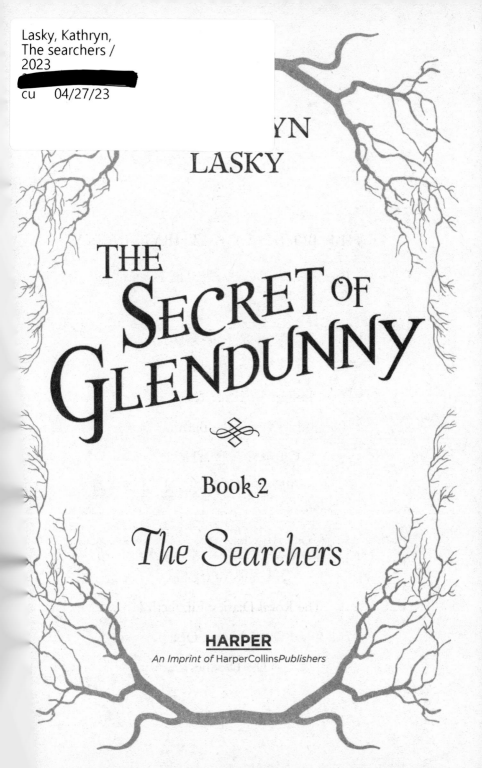

KATHRYN
LASKY

THE SECRET OF GLENDUNNY

Book 2

The Searchers

HARPER
An Imprint of HarperCollinsPublishers

To Christopher Knight,
always in my lodge and by my side.

CONTENTS

Inlet Stream

Dam 3

Locksley's Lodge

Was Heath

Lower Scum

Yrynn's Lodge

GLENDUNNY

N
W · E
S

PART ONE

Feathers Lost

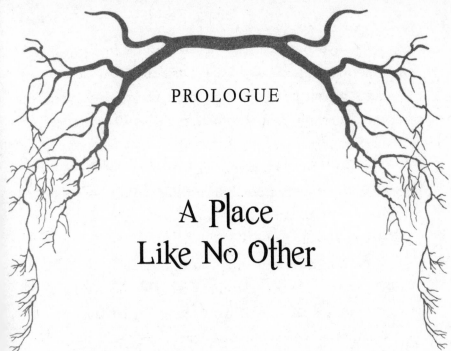

PROLOGUE

A Place Like No Other

"The beaver is coming to, Doc. Breathing normalized. I think another dose and he'll regain consciousness."

"But how soon will he be trainable? The wolves did quite a bit of damage to some of his muscle tissue."

None of these words made any sense at all to Levi. But, unfortunately, one thing did make sense. These were human voices. Even if he did not understand all of the words, the noises were the sounds that two-legs made. That hadn't been the intention when he had joined the rebel beavers in Glendunny to take over the pond. He was the youngest in the rebellion, hoping to impress Retta, a lovely young beaver kit. To be part of this rebellion sounded so exciting, so impressive. But where had it landed him? In captivity in this weird place called New Eden and controlled by humans! Human beings, of all creatures. The whole purpose of the Glendunny pond was to keep the beavers' existence a secret from humans.

"A coup," the old beaver Snert had called the rebellion. Snert felt that he had been unfairly deprived of his rights to become their leader, the Castor Aquarius of the pond of Glendunny.

Levi himself was uncertain about this. He knew little of the politics of the Glendunny pond. He simply wanted to improve his status. And volunteering for the dangerous mission was a way he might advance. But now, he had no idea whatsoever where he was. Yet he had the dreadful realization that he was among humans in some sort of pond that was not a pond—no mud, no weed, no slime or scum. The sides were very smooth and for the most part transparent. There was a sign with letters: POOL 53.

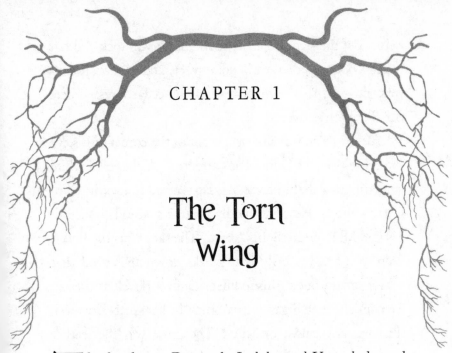

CHAPTER 1

The Torn Wing

The three beavers *Dunwattle, Locksley, and Yrynn had stared* into the chasm where the bodies of their enemies lay. "This is the canyon of the dead," the Rar Wolf Nyarr had said. "It is not heaven. It is not *feasghair*, where some souls often wander endlessly. It is Nothingness. This is their hell. Nothingness."

And since that moment when Nyarr had spoken, a moon had risen, and the three exhausted beaver kits had slept. Near dawn they began to stir. Dunwattle was the first to rouse. He broke from his slumber and, after giving himself a good shake, stretched his front legs and his back ones. Then he waddled off a short distance and gave a good slap of his tail, as was the custom of most beavers upon rising. But the slap had a flat sound, for it was rock and not water—not the pond of Glendunny. He and his two friends were now on this high plateau of the cedar forest, where the Rar Wolves lived.

Although he was still sleepy, out of the corner of his eye something caught Dunwattle's attention. A flutter of white quivering in a slight breeze. A gasp seemed to lock in Dunwattle's throat. He could hardly breathe as dread flashed in his gut. More precisely his "skeat." The skeat was the pouch deep in a beaver's belly that breaks down the wood that beavers gnaw. But at this moment Dunwattle felt as if there were an entire undigested tree stuck in his skeat. However, this was not caused by wood. The cause was the feather he spotted. A swan feather with a stain of blood trembled in the breeze. Dunwattle began to tremble all over, and he could not tear his eyes from the fragile plume.

"What are you shaking about? Are you having a . . . a fit?" It was Locksley. "Oh, Great Castor!" Locksley exclaimed as the realization of what he was seeing dawned on him. "That's . . . that's . . ."

"Elsinore's feather," Dunwattle replied weakly.

"Filoplume, port wing." Locksley almost choked on his own words. "You know what this means?" Dunwattle wasn't certain, but Locksley most likely knew for sure. Locksley had become obsessed with the plumage of swans. He knew more than any non-flying creature about feathers of swans and other birds as well. They weren't just simply feathers to Locksley. There were so many kinds—primaries, secondaries, lesser coverts, medium coverts, greater coverts, and tiny feathers called winglets.

"Elsinore! She's been wounded," Dunwattle cried. It was unthinkable that the First Swan of Glendunny pond, who served as protector and defender of the pond and constantly flew out on surveillance flights to scout for humans, had been part of this battle that was nowhere near them. How had this happened? "There is blood on that filoplume. I didn't even know she was here during the battle." Elsinore herself was their friend, their guide, whom they confided in and who had sworn never to betray their secrets. Although Elsinore was a swan and about as different as a creature could be from their own species, in many ways they felt closer to Elsinore than to their own parents.

"I didn't know she was here either." Locksley sighed. "But this is bad. Very bad, Dunwattle."

"But Locksley, it's just a small feather."

"Doesn't matter. Filoplumes are attached to nerve endings and if they are damaged—oh Great Castor! They are vital to flying and insulation. They are used in course corrections all the time."

"But they can regrow them, right?" Suddenly Dunwattle froze.

"What is it, Dunwattle?" Locksley followed Dunwattle's

gaze. Sticking up right in the crack of a rock was the shaft of the white primary feather.

"She's doomed!" Dunwattle gasped. "Elsinore is doomed!"

"No!" said a voice behind them. It was Yrynn. "We just have to find her. She might not be in flight, but we have to find her. We . . . we . . . ," Yrynn stammered. "We have to follow the feathers."

"Follow the bloodstains, you mean." Dunwattle now wailed and began wildly slapping his tail on the rock plateau.

Yrynn wheeled about and sat up straight on her own broad tail. "Stop this sniveling and wailing! We don't know she's dead. It's not winter yet. She won't need the insulation."

"But for guidance, small adjustments—flight feathers and their coverts are essential for fine trimming a swan's flight. She won't be able to go where she wants to go." Locksley was bawling now.

"Pull yourself together, Locksley," Yrynn scolded. Sometimes Locksley's deep knowledge of feathers could be extremely annoying.

"She won't go anywhere if she's dead, Yrynn!" Dunwattle snapped. There was a clack of his two large bright orange front teeth.

"Dunwattle, Locksley, let's be practical, we have to follow her."

"Follow her?" Locksley asked.

"Follow the path of blood and feathers."

And so they did. The feathers came mostly one by one. But sometimes there were two or three. And there were often stains of blood on the leaves of low-growing bushes or rocks. But what the three beaver kits most dreaded was finding the long, sweeping primary flight feathers with their broad shafts. Those tended to leave a lot of blood on the ground. The kits had lost track of time but not track of the feathers of Elsinore, their beloved Elsinore, First Swan of the pond of Glendunny—their mentor, their teacher, their finest friend.

Elsinore was descended from the original First Swan, Byatta of Great Fosters, in the time of King Henry VIII, also known to the beavers as Big Hank. It was Byatta who was dispatched by Avalinda, the Aquarius of the Great Fosters pond, who had discovered the pond of Glendunny far to the north in Scotland. The beavers had decided to flee from the king, because he had a dangerous appetite for them. Not just their meat, but their fur as well, to be used for clothing. Since that time, every other swan of Glendunny had descended from the Byatta ancestral line.

The savagery of the king, Big Hank, knew no bounds. He was a monarch who dined on beaver meat and loved nothing more than having their pelts for trimming capes and turning the leftovers into his jaunty hats and mufflers.

The sight of this brutal monarch with his bristly red beard nestled in the fur collar made of Avalinda's own mate's pelt was truly nauseating. But it could not compare to the day when Avalinda lost her firstborn kit, Abby, to Big Hank. He had murdered the young one and had her pelt turned into a cloak and adorable hat with little flaps, all to warm the ears of his daughter the princess.

That was the last chip for Avalinda. She consulted Byatta, then ordered the First Swan to fly out and look for another pond as far away as possible from the king's hunting lodge. A pond that no two-leg would be tempted to go near.

So it came to pass that on the fifth day of Byatta's journey she looked down and saw what appeared to be a long-abandoned village, with a stream flowing through the very center. *Extremely dammable!* The words surged through her mind. She could picture it now. And there were other water resources nearby that with the right engineering could be channeled into the pond. In no time at all the beavers of Great Fosters could have a new pond, with the promise of expanding it.

It was on this first visit when she found the myriad of bones—bones of two-legs—that Byatta figured out why this village had been abandoned. "Haunted!" she murmured to herself, as she came upon the shoulder bone of a small two-leg—a child who had been murdered. Additional research proved Byatta's theory right. There had been a king in those long-ago days, more than a century before Big Hank, who was even more savage than Henry VIII. His name was King Edward, or Edward Longshanks, due to his very long legs. It was Edward Longshanks who had wreaked death—a massacre—upon this village in his attempts to become the king of Scotland. No human dared come near the place.

After several years of diligent work by the beavers and the construction of highly sophisticated dams, the water rose and drowned out the village and all the bones of the murdered two-legs who had inhabited it. In the minds of the two-legs, it was a cursed and haunted village. No one wanted to come close to it. Isolated from two-legs, the beavers could work in peace, and gradually, as the waters rose, it was forgotten that the village of Glendunny ever existed. The massacre by King Edward was the origin of how this idyllic pond came to be. But through the years, the beavers were determined that only a few of the highest-ranking members of their governing body, the Castorium, would know the dark history from which their pond had been born. It was the Secret of Glendunny. Unfortunately, the kits had learned the story of the massacre through the accidental encounter that poor Dunwattle had with a wandering ghost of a murdered child, Lorna Fitzhugh. And what Lorna had not told them, Elsinore had filled in with the gruesome details. Elsinore did not believe in hiding things from young beavers when their own safety was at stake.

Now the last feather that the kits found was on the banks of a river beneath a rocky ledge. "This is the place," Dunwattle said mournfully as they huddled and peered down at yet another feather.

"What do you mean?" Locksley asked. "You mean the place where Elsinore was murdered?"

"Locksley," Yrynn said in a scolding voice, "don't jump to conclusions. Do you see a body here?" She didn't wait for an answer. "No, of course you don't." She turned now to Dunwattle. She felt she knew what he was about to say.

"This is the place where I was first seen by a two-leg, a human being." Dunwattle could hardly get the words out. "First and only time, please! My crime of *vysculf*! It happened here. Right here!" Dunwattle stomped his front paw.

Indeed, that had been when all their troubles had begun. A few treacherous beavers of the pond had set a band, or a curse, of lynx on Dunwattle. If it hadn't been for that, the kits would have never been attacked in the cedar woods. Elsinore would have never been wounded, and they would have all lived happily ever after. But that was not to be.

And the kits could not imagine a pond, a world, without their beloved Elsinore.

"But Dunwattle," Yrynn said, "do you think it's safe for us to come back here? They might still be looking about for beavers here."

The scene blazed in Dunwattle's mind of those dreadful moments. The woman on the embankment with her camera. The terrible flash of light. The blinding paralysis when the world went white, an electrical white like during a summer storm. And then the bespectacled lady on the banks exclaiming, *My! My! My! I can hardly believe my eyes. A beaver! A beaver in England!* There had not been one seen for centuries.

Like a bad dream, it came back to him. Yrynn extended her paw. She hadn't meant to upset him so.

"Now, Dunwattle. Calm down. We're well hidden . . . and you know this is where the feathers have led us. How many did we find just today?"

"Twenty or thirty," Locksley said mournfully. "It's amazing she has any left to fly with!" he added bitterly.

"But fly she has!" Dunwattle said, seeming to have recovered. "There is no denying it. She certainly hasn't walked this far!"

Locksley dared not speak what he was thinking—that in fact there was plenty to deny it. Elsinore's body could be on some trash heap somewhere! One of the dumps that she herself used to scour in order to find treasures for the ridiculous Castor Aquarius, the governor of the pond. When elected the Aquarius, this once modest beaver, Oscar of Was Meadow, became obsessed with "royalty" and changed his formal title from Castor Aquarius to G. A., which stood for Grand Aquarius. Oscar of Was Meadow had arrived at this lofty position by accident after the previous leader, the lovely wise beaver Wanda, had been murdered by a curse of lynx.

In any case, this new Aquarius had an unhealthy fondness for the castoffs of two-legs. So, he often dispatched Elsinore on aerial surveillance missions. The purpose of these missions was not simply to gain weather information, or signs of human occupation moving in too close to the remote region of Glendunny pond, but to scour dumps for what the new Aquarius considered treasures. She brought back paper crowns from the King Burger fast-food restaurants that the Aquarius regarded as real and most splendid. At one point he was even wielding a toilet plunger as his scepter.

But what did Oscar of Was Meadow know of toilets or crowns for that matter? He was, or had been, a simple fellow before he became the Aquarius. An exceptional bark stripper with a true talent of predicting the swell rates of logs. Some speculated that something happened to him during the earthquake that occurred shortly after he became the

Aquarius. That perhaps he had been hit on the head by a falling rock or a tree.

"How long have we been gone now since the disaster in the cedar forest?" Locksley asked. "Do you think we can return?"

"You mean can I return? Is there still a price on my head for committing vysculf? I am the one guilty of the worst crime in Glendunny—being seen by a two-leg."

"By now things must have changed, Dunwattle," Locksley said. "The devils who led that craziness, the ones who set a price on your head—Tonk, Carrick, Snert, and that dimwit Levi—are all dead, including the curse of lynx they set upon you. I think it would be safe now."

"I suppose so," Dunwattle mused. "And I guess our parents must be missing us."

"Of course," Locksley replied. "My mum must be hysterical with grief and my da too, tearing his fur out, I think." He sighed wearily as he thought of the anguish his parents must be suffering.

Yrynn remained silent. There was no one who was missing her. Her parents had vanished the summer before the earthquake, and as a beaver whose family had Canadian origins, albeit centuries ago, she was considered by the snobbish beavers of the pond to be something slightly lesser. But who would miss her? Yrynn wondered. Only those who now huddled close to her, beneath the rock ledge of the riverbank—and of course Lorna. Lorna was the only two-leg she knew, but Lorna nevertheless was a ghost. Murdered more than seven hundred years ago in the massacre of Glendunny, Lorna had finally, blessedly, found Neamorra, the Gaelic word for heaven. That was where Lorna belonged, with the two-leg ghosts, but where did she, Yrynn, belong?

CHAPTER 2

Two Old Spies
and a Wounded Swan

W *here am I, exactly? Elsinore wondered. Where have I been for* the last three days? She knew she had been wounded badly. The paralyzing, terrible green light, the evil light that emanated from the eyes of the lynx, was unforgettable. It felt as if her own eyes had been scalded, yet she could not shut them. It was the lynx—their peculiar way of transfixing their victims. They had done significant damage to her port wing, but somehow, she had broken out of the evil web of light and risen—bloody and determined. "*Svanka velsignet,*" she murmured. It was a blessing, a blessing in the language of Old Swan.

She was unsure of where she was or had been. But at this moment, even though she was not flying, it seemed as if she were drafting in the wake of a larger and more powerful swan. Yet at the same time she felt immobilized in some strange way, as though she were floating winglessly. She sensed that she was wrapped in something rather tight. Her port wing was immobilized in what she thought might be what two-legs called a splint. Her leg was bandaged as well. She lay on soft padding.

She gradually realized that she had been moved from one kind of a two-leg nest, or home, to another that was not actually a home at all. She saw that she was in a conveyance of some sort. Unlike beavers, Elsinore was thoroughly familiar with modern conveyances, because of her far-reaching surveillance flights for the pond. So, although her mind was slightly muddled from her grievous wounds, she attempted now to clarify her thoughts through a process of elimination. Hopefully she could in this way figure out where she was. *Automobile—no. Truck—no. Train—no. Could it be—oh please, Svanka, no!* But it was an airplane! Not a jet, *not a helicopter—oh Svanka, forgive, not a helicopter!* What helicopters did to air was unspeakable. They chopped up the air, mangled currents and the clouds, leaving confusing contrails—streaks—in their wake. In short, they deformed the sky.

But as she listened to the engine and glanced around, she realized that this was a small plane—most likely a Piper Cherokee. Single engine, fixed landing gear. It could fly at a speed of approximately 160 miles per hour. At least five times her own cruising speed.

"I think she's coming to or realizes she's not still on land back at Skibodeen," a voice croaked.

"Good," said another voice.

Elsinore had a better view of the second voice. It was the pilot. A rather elderly-looking two-leg.

"Looks like it's going to have to be an instrument approach to Little Feidah Island," said the male voice. "Sorry I can't help you, but I want to keep the fluids going. She needs fluids."

"Don't worry, Lachlan. I've got this under control."

"Never doubted it for a second. I remember that landing you made behind the enemy lines in Belgium."

"Ha! That was a million years ago."

"Not quite but close. World War Two. November thirtieth 1944. What was it, two weeks before the Battle of the Bulge?"

"Sounds about right to me."

"Not many of the female pilots were flying sorties."

"A few of us were. Loved that little Spitfire I flew."

"How long has your pilot's license been out of date?"

"Oh my, I don't know. Maybe forty years or so. What about you?"

"At least fifty!"

"Well, no one checks on Little Feidah—I own the island. So, I make the rules."

Little Feidah! Elsinore knew exactly where that was—an island in the Minch, the straits in the northern Hebrides. Little Feidah Island was part of an archipelago off the west coast of Scotland. This group of islands was on a flight track to the sea of Wyntersphree, Elsinore's own home where she had hatched in the far north. Uninhabited and on no one's flight course, really. *So, this is where they are taking me!* she thought.

"I'm telling you I'm happy this cloud bank has settled upon us. I nearly had a heart attack when that niece of mine started talking about drones and putting one of those GPF gadgets on some swan's ankle."

"Well, Glencora, I believe the term is GPS—global positioning system."

"Whatever! But if she had put that darned device on it, she believed this swan might lead her to find that damn beaver she spotted on the Tweed River. Now mind you, Lachlan, I have nothing against beavers, and Lord knows I have nothing against swans. I know their cohabiting tradition, or I guess it's called symbiotic living arrangements. Good for both species. But I don't like it when humans start interfering. Oh, I know, it's all in the name of science. Yet I should have thought more about this when my niece

Adelaide got obsessed with that beaver she glimpsed. I'm ashamed to say that I helped pay for some of her research." Glencora Barrington sighed. "But honestly, three months ago I was an innocent. I thought it would just be a lot of professors tromping around with binoculars, but not these drones and GPF thing—sorry, GPS things." She was muttering now. "No one uses words anymore, just initials. Shakespeare must be turning in his grave."

"I use words, Glencora. You use words."

"I know, schnooks." She reached with one long, very thin arm and ruffled the few strands of hair on Lachlan's mostly bald head. "That's why I'm so fond of you, dear." She sighed. "Now before I land this jalopy recite that poem for me again."

Oh, please no, Elsinore thought. That foolish poem. But it was too late, as Lachlan MacLean in his thick brogue began reciting the Orlando Gibbons poem written hundreds of years before.

The silver swan, who living had no note,
When death approached, unlocked her silent throat.
Leaning her breast against the reedy shore,
Thus sung her first and last, and sung no more:
"Farewell, all joys; O death, come close mine eyes.
More geese than swans now live, more fools than wise."

Elsinore let loose with an explosive snort of disgust that was halfway between a gasp and a growl.

"Well, well," Lachlan said. "Our patient seems to be on the road to recovery, Glencora."

"It's a complete myth about mute swans not making sounds. And certainly not when they are about to take their last breath," Glencora Barrington said over her shoulder.

Thank you, Miss Glencora, whoever you are. Thank you for helping to destroy that myth about the muteness of my species. But please, no more poetry!

CHAPTER 3

Unsung Heroes

The three beaver kits, *Locksley, Dunwattle, and Yrynn, looked* about in awe. They could hardly believe it—they were perched on their tails at the very center of the lodge of the Castor Castorium, the most hallowed of Glendunny pond, where the Aquarius dwelled. It was only to these select few members who constituted the council of the Castorium that the secret history and origins of the pond had been revealed. It was in the Castorium where the laws of the pond were made. However, it was not only laws, but also where strategies for engineering and new construction of dams were discussed and often argued about. The Castorium was the beating heart of Glendunny.

Now, however, the hearts of the three beavers were

beating thunderously in their own ears. Never before had young beaver kits been allowed to enter. And their elders were waiting for them. What amazed the kits most was the transformation in their leader, the Aquarius, Oscar of Was Meadow. Gone were his royal trimmings—the crown he used to wear as he paddled about the pond. Nor was there any sign of his scepter. The scepter that was rumored to be a device for plunging the waste of two-legs down mechanical buckets called toilets. Not a trace of the dangly jewels—the bling, as Elsinore often called those tawdry gems that the Aquarius often adorned himself with. This Aquarius was now a sober and very serious beaver. He was also clearly grieving, as were all the members of the Castorium. For they were grieving the loss of their beloved swan Elsinore.

"We've called you here," the Aquarius of the pond began, "first to apologize." He turned toward Dunwattle and nodded. "Yes, Dunwattle, you were seen. You were accused of the most serious crime of the Castorium, of vysculf—to be seen by two-legs, or humans, as they call themselves. It must have been an accident."

"Oh, it was, sir, it most certainly was."

The Aquarius held up his paw. "We believe you. There is no need to convince us. But we still need to apologize, as some treacherous members of our community—Carrick, Snert of the Snout, Castor Tonk, and young Levi—had joined with a vile curse of lynx to try to kill you. The same curse of lynx who assassinated my predecessor and your own grandmother, Wanda the Wattler. Though their actions were unforgivable, they have met their justifiable deaths."

The three kits gasped. "B-b-but . . . but . . ." Locksley's mouth seemed unable to find the shape of the words. "How do you know this?" he finally blurted out.

"The eagles of Iolaire."

In the minds of the beaver kits, the eagles of Iolaire were almost a fabled species. With wingspans of nearly ten feet, they were the largest eagles in the world. Rarely seen but rumored to be as expert as Elsinore in flying surveillance.

"The eagles," Yrynn gasped.

"You saw them?" Locksley asked.

"I can't believe it," Dunwattle blurted. "How did this happen? Where? When?"

"They came to us," the Aquarius said.

"They came to you!" Locksley said. His eyes were wide with disbelief, for this was unheard of.

"They witnessed your bravery," Castor Elwyn said. Elwyn was one of the kits' favorite teachers. He was the Castor of water dynamics and hydrology. "But they arrived too late to help."

"Did they see what happened to Elsinore?" Dunwattle asked desperately. "She was wounded. We are certain. We found several of her feathers."

"They did not mention this at all. They certainly would have told us if they had seen her."

"We tried so hard to track her," Yrynn said. "But then the trail of bloody feathers just disappeared."

"It could have been the wind," the Aquarius replied. "The wind could have swept through and stirred the feathers every which way. But no, the eagles did not see what might have happened to Elsinore." Then the Aquarius slid his eyes toward others in the Castorium. It appeared as if a message had silently passed between him and the other Castors. "It seems that the traitorous beavers who attacked you with the lynx were killed by you and the Rar Wolves." The Aquarius paused a long time. He looked toward Elwyn, who looked toward Kukla, the librarian, and they both nodded. "Yes, Tonk, Snert, Carrick, along with the curse of lynx, were all killed except one."

"Who was that?" Locksley asked, stepping forward.

"Levi."

"Levi, that wipsnizzle," Dunwattle exclaimed.

Wipsnizzle was one of the worst things a young beaver could call another. If they were heard using that despicable word, they were often severely punished. But no one said a word until the Aquarius himself muttered, "I entirely agree. 'Wipsnizzle.'" He now took a deep breath. "The eagles have reported that Levi was seriously wounded and taken to the far north, to an island in the region of the ice floes. This island is a secret to most of the world but controlled by evil two-legs."

Yrynn now stepped forward. She was the smallest of the kits, and her pelt was a lighter color that was almost bronze. As a Canuck beaver from Canada, she had been looked down upon by others of the pond. Added to that was the fact that she was an orphan. But things had changed now. The Aquarius seemed to have paid special attention to Yrynn, as if he were addressing her in some way in particular.

"Yes, Yrynn, you have a question?"

"What exactly is it that you are asking us to do? Because I think that is why you called us here. Not merely to tell us we were brave."

The Aquarius sighed. He realized what a perceptive kit this young one was. "We believe that Levi is not the only creature from this pond who is there, but possibly our beloved Elsinore too."

"What?" all three kits said at once.

"Why there, to the far north?" Locksley asked in a rather demanding voice. "The feathers we tracked were to the south and west."

"Was it the eagles who said this?" Yrynn interrupted. "Did they tell you something?"

"Not precisely." Elwyn now spoke. "But they found some

feathers too." He paused a long time. "You know, young'uns, water dynamics and wind dynamics are not all that different. There are currents of air that stir things up just as the way-back eddies swirl in reverse in a river. If you can read the wind the way these eagles do . . ." Elwyn paused. "Well, the eagles believe that Elsinore might be there as well. And perhaps an eagle too. These evil people have a fascination with creatures, creatures of all species that they can train, mold, and brainwash to do their evil work."

"And what is this place called?" Yrynn took a step closer.

"The Dark Place," the Aquarius replied. He hesitated a bit. "And some call it New Eden."

"Why?" Locksley asked. The Aquarius and Kukla the librarian exchanged a quick glance.

"We're not sure," the Aquarius answered quickly. Too quickly, Locksley noticed. This was the way it was with grown-ups sometimes. They weren't lying exactly, but they just wanted to avoid answering. *Not for young ears*, he recalled his mum often saying. And yet these young ears had already heard and seen terrible things. They deserved a better answer. But he would not push it. Perhaps Elwyn would tell them.

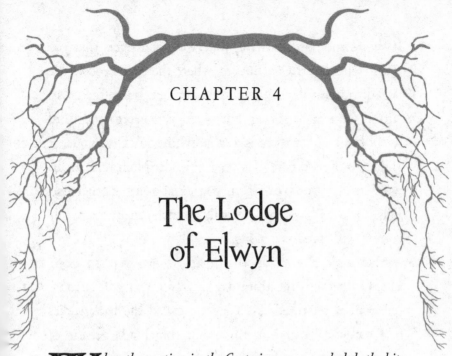

CHAPTER 4

The Lodge
of Elwyn

When the meeting in the Castorium was concluded, the kits followed Castor Elwyn to his lodge in Was Heath. It was a cozy lodge crammed with old books, volumes with titles such as *Waterways of Great Britain*, *Hydrology Through the Ages*, *Applied Hydrology*, *General Introduction to Hydraulics*, and *Water Currents in Rivers and Streams*. Every wall of the lodge was covered with maps and charts that recorded the water tables of the pond of Glendunny, meticulously updated with each season.

There was never much idle chitchat with Elwyn. He plunged right into the subject matter.

"Here you see a very detailed map that our dear Elsinore scavenged for me from the Bristol Academy of Hydraulics.

It shows the north-flowing waterways and rivers that you must swim to arrive at Iolaire, where the eagles roost." He began to point to one map, then another. "Here the cross-currents are quite strong, but when you get to the third set of back eddies there is a large whirlpool. Dive under it and cross over to here." He used a slender birch limb as his pointer. "And you'll be fine if you surface on the other side. Plus, the whirlpool will actually funnel you into a lovely current and speed you along."

He next put up another map. "Now step up close, kits. On perhaps the third day of travel, you will encounter another set of eddies. They are called the back eddies of Pynchyndalia. It is at this point you should get out of the river and proceed on land. There are some very violent waterfalls. Best to avoid them or get smashed to furry bits at the bottom of the falls."

Lovely, thought Locksley. But he said nothing.

Elwyn turned around now and faced the kits. "Any questions?" Yrynn raised a paw. "Yes, Yrynn."

"But what are our chances of being seen by two-legs, the chances of vysculf?"

"Interesting question, my dear."

Interesting! Yrynn thought. *It's our lives!* The same thought was passing through the minds of both Locksley and Dun-wattle.

"It seems although our pond at Glendunny has been

avoided by two-legs for many centuries because of the horrendous massacre that came to pass here long ago, these northern regions have also been avoided, for different reasons."

"Not a massacre, then, no ghosts?" Dunwattle recalled the ghost of Lorna that had frightened him so badly that it caused him to bolt from his lodge and be seen by that two-leg on the river.

"No, no ghosts at all. It is the eagles who have frightened off human settlement there," Elwyn said.

"Why?" Locksley asked.

"They are enormous. They are fierce. They think nothing of plunging down and picking off a lamb or even a small cow, or perhaps even a little two-leg human." Elwyn scratched his head. "Now what do they call those?"

"Children," Yrynn answered solemnly.

"Yes, children," he replied.

Now Locksley raised his hand.

"Yes, Locksley?"

"I have a question, sir."

"Yes?"

"Why do they call the Dark Place New Eden?"

"Uh . . ." The elderly beaver began to tremble a bit. "I . . . uh . . . really can't answer that." He took a deep breath. "But you best be on your way, kits . . . on your way." He tried to muster a sprightly tone in his voice. "Off you go."

When they left the lodge of Elwyn, there was a chill in the air as the first of the Hunger Moons rose. Soon there would be a thin skim of ice on the pond—just as last year when the terrible earthquake had happened. As they climbed over Dam 3 and slipped into the inlet stream, each kit was alone with their thoughts. Locksley was trying to conjure up in his imagination what these eagles might look like. But they were unimaginable, with their massive wingspans that were as broad as the dam they had just scrambled over.

Dunwattle's parents had tied a small good-luck charm to his hind paw. "Don't worry, dear," his mum had said. "It won't interfere with your swimming. In fact, I think it helps it. You feel its tickle and you know you have picked up a subcurrent."

The good-luck charm seemed so silly. He didn't even want to have to explain it to the others. It was embarrassing. And he felt sorry for poor Yrynn—an orphan. Who had said goodbye to her? Who had stroked her lovely golden pelt and told her to stay safe? The thought of Yrynn being so alone almost crushed him. Yes, she had Dunwattle and Locksley as friends, but no one who would give her a good-luck charm. There was no one to squeeze and hug her as Locksley's parents had done to the point of embarrassment when he left his lodge to join them. Yes, it was embarrassing, but still, you knew that someone would be thinking of you. But who was thinking of Yrynn? Well, he was, for one.

Dunwattle had to admit that he was just a bit in love with her. He secretly wrote poems about her. But honestly, Dunwattle thought, she had to be the loneliest beaver in the pond. He would always recall that night when he'd helped Yrynn move the log downstream. She did what Canadian beavers did best—which was to "dance" a log against the current. He remembered how the river in the light of a full moon was like a sparkling ribbon of jewels, and Yrynn with her golden pelt shone as she danced the log upstream. Every step dainty and elegant! She cast a silhouette against the silvered water of the river. And now Dunwattle recalled the mother otter from that evening with her adorable baby otters. That now seemed so long ago. The pups had been cradled on her stomach as she drifted by. Dunwattle recalled thinking that otters definitely had more fun than beavers. With beavers it was all work, no play. Just work work work! But otters were different. They played—they tossed river muck and played catch games with rocks. They performed fancy dives. He wondered where that otter and her pups might be now. Were they still in the river, or perhaps they had swum off to another? Dunwattle would have loved to learn their catch games. He wanted to learn how to play, rather than just work all the time.

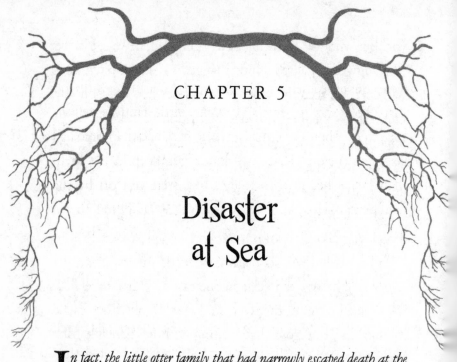

CHAPTER 5

Disaster at Sea

In fact, the little otter family that had narrowly escaped death at the claws and fangs of the vicious lynx Grinfyll had been at sea for nearly a week. They were doing well, and Glory looked with pride at her two pups, Iglemore and Edlmyn. They had become good little swimmers—ocean swimmers, saltwater swimmers—though they had been born river otters. But in the tangled history of sea otters and river otters on this earth, there was a time called the mustah when all species of otters were one. Then there had been no divisions between the otters of rivers and those of sea, no difference between clear and salt water.

Through some ancient instinct, Glory had guided her pups toward the large back eddies of the legendary Gulf

Stream. It was strong and powerful and could drag them too far south, away from their destination—Canada. But there were counter-eddies, and these were the swirling whirlpools that Glory was in search of for her little family's deliverance to the shores of Canada, where her ancestral home had been eons before. There was something deep in her brain that guided her to these eddies that were cast off by the Gulf Stream. How lucky they had been so far. Often, they'd hardly had to swim at all. And if a large patch of kelp or seaweed would float by, they would climb on top of it.

The floating mattresses were rich in food—small fish like sardines and herring that had become snagged in the briny tangles, along with mollusks that they could crack with their back teeth. Squid were their favorite, and they often swam up to the surface and were easily snagged. But sometimes the otters did miss the crisp, fresh taste of a river trout.

"I really could use a nice bite of pink perch. Remember how good the Tweed River ones were, Mum?" Iglemore asked.

"Eat that periwinkle. This lovely mattress is simply crawling with snails, and they are delicious."

"They're so tiny and they take forever to pick out. I think I swallowed one with the shell the other day."

"I'm sure it came out the other end, Edy, so stop complaining."

"Shark alert!" Iglemore called out. A fin sliced through the cold green waters of the Atlantic.

"Stay calm, pup. No paws dangling over the side of our sea mat."

Glory prayed that the waters would not roughen. It was because it was so calm in this part that they had spied the fin. She thought it was a great white, as she could see its tail now and it was quite a distance from that dorsal fin. The great whites were among the largest of sharks. She prayed that this patch of seaweed they were floating on would not disintegrate, as the next patch that she could spot was some distance away. If they slipped into the water, the shark would pick up their scent. Were the pups fast enough to get to it? She was fast, but if she swam with them on her belly, that would slow her down considerably. The shark came closer and seemed to tip to one side. His huge iridescent blue eye rolled up. It was truly enormous. But now the eyeball seemed to turn white. *It's attacking!*

Glory hugged her pups to her side. The placid sea began to rock, and there was a tumult of breaking water over the mat of seaweed and wild gusts of wind. Through it all a deafening noise. This was not a shark but something else entirely. A beast from the sky was descending.

The last thing Glory remembered was that she and the pups were not in the sea but in some kind of net, dangling above the sea. When she looked down, she saw the shark cruise off serenely into the flat waters where calm had been restored. But above the otters, metal blades chopped the air and there were puffy clouds oblivious to the roar of the churning flying machine that had snagged the otters in its net.

Then she heard a crackling and a voice—a human voice, or a two-leg, as the beavers called such creatures.

"Mission control, this is chopper five-eight-three Juliet. Heading to base with three otters. They look like river otters, but they were out here at latitude fifty-nine north by eleven west."

"Preparing pool fifty-four with mixed saline solution."

"Arrival at oh six hundred."

"Good going, Bruce. Over and out."

The otter pups were mewling and pressed themselves against their mum. *This is the end*, thought Glory. *The end*.

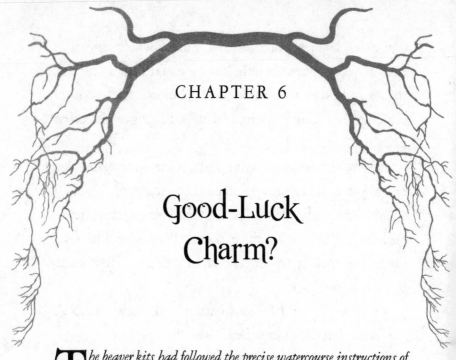

CHAPTER 6

Good-Luck Charm?

The beaver kits had followed the precise watercourse instructions of Castor Elwyn. Indeed, they were ahead of schedule. They had negotiated the first set of crosscurrents by the dawn of their second day. Now the third set of crosscurrents was behind them, as they had dived deep under the large whirlpool as Elwyn had instructed. They had hardly felt its violence and had emerged safely on the other side. Then they were swiftly funneled into a lovely current that sped them along with no effort on their part whatsoever. The beaver kits even rolled on their backs and tried to imitate those otters who often cruised on their backs and juggled small rocks. The kits were good at cruising on their backs but poor at juggling.

Perhaps Dunwattle was distracted by thoughts of the juggling otters, because he quickly realized he had been snagged by a powerful surge in the river. There was no one around him. Instead, he saw his two friends Locksley and Yrynn were screaming and barking from shore, where Elwyn had instructed them to get out. But their barks were soon drowned out by the rush of the falls.

Oh, Great Castor, I missed the turnoff. I am going over the falls . . . ! He felt the lucky charm tickling against his foot, as if mocking him. *Some good luck this is!*

On shore, Locksley and Yrynn were transfixed as they watched the tiny body of their friend devoured by the great maw of the falls. The noise of the powerful falls was thunderous. The jagged rocks below spiked from the boiling water like the teeth of the fiercest monster. There was no way that Dunwattle could survive. Locksley and Yrynn clung to each other in horror and fear as they watched their friend. It was as if a vital part of them had been ripped from their own bodies. But in truth it was Dunwattle who would be ripped apart—they couldn't stand it.

Somehow the two beavers stumbled along the route that Elwyn had shown them on the map. There would be a calm stretch of the river soon. They would reenter the river and look for what remained of their dear friend. But there was simply no chance that he could have survived this. None at all.

The roar of the falls began to recede, and they had not gone far when they saw something in the choppy water.

"What is that?" Locksley said, squinting.

"Logs, I think," Yrynn said.

"But very odd logs," Locksley replied.

Yrynn caught her breath. "Yes, very odd logs." In fact, these logs seemed familiar in some way. She scrambled up onto a high bank for a better view.

"I can't believe it!" she gasped.

"What?"

"Une creuse!"

"A what?" Locksley asked.

"A dugout . . . a French canoe."

"I don't understand," Locksley said.

"It's a kind of boat . . . Canadian beavers learned how to gnaw them, hollow them out, and even make paddles, and . . . and . . . Locksley, those beavers in them are Canucks! Look at their pelts! They are paddling toward that lumpy thing floating in the water."

"What lumpy thing?"

"It's Dunwattle!"

"Is he alive?"

That was Locksley's first question as they swam up to

the dugout paddled by three large golden beavers. The third paddler in the stern of the boat was steering with his large broad tail. Yrynn was too stunned to speak. How could this be? How could there be Canadian beavers here? She followed in a trance as the canoe made its way to the banks of the river. Her mum had told her about the New World beavers of Canada and the strange boats called "creuse." But it was so unbelievable. So mythic, like the star stories and legends her mum told her of the constellations.

"He lives!" said a somewhat grizzled old beaver who paddled from the bow of the canoe. His golden fur was threaded with white. It looked as if he had been caught in a sudden snowstorm, but it was not snow. In fact, a drizzling cold rain had begun.

On shore, a sled woven out of stripped alder branches and lined with moss was waiting. Two large burly beavers hoisted Dunwattle onto the sled. The kits gasped as they saw that his fur was streaked with blood.

"It's a travois," Yrynn murmured to herself. This was another contraption that her mum and da had told her about. *Mum and Da.* The two words echoed now in her ears along with her mum's voice. *If we were in Canada, you would call us Maman and Père.* A deep yearning seized Yrynn as she whispered the two words to herself. How she longed to say those two lovely soft words, to speak them out loud. What she would not give to nestle into their golden fur. She looked about. She was now surrounded by creatures with golden fur. But none were her parents. Would the missing ever stop?

The Canadian beavers, Yrynn's mother had told her, had learned about travois from the Indigenous people, or the "naturals," as the beavers had called them in that distant land. No one noticed, but Yrynn was completely spellbound now by these glimpses of a world she had only heard of but never knew. A world that she thought was lost.

Locksley looked down at his dear friend Dunwattle. "Is he alive?"

CHAPTER 7

A New Language That Is Very Old

"He is breathing, although raggedly," said an elderly beaver. "I think with a dose of betula we can mend this poor kit."

"Betula?" Yrynn asked. "You mean birch."

"Yes, yes. Birch water is the best thing for these injuries, stops the bleeding quickly." The beaver now called out, "Betula! Betula! Emergency. Beaver went over the falls. Badly wounded."

Locksley and Yrynn looked at each other with astonishment. What in the world? Was this beaver calling a birch tree to come to poor Dunwattle's side and release its sap? This indeed would be magical—a walking birch tree!

A very plump beaver soon waddled out from a grove

of pines. She carried two satchels strapped across her shoulders and wore a colorful bandanna, as the two-legs called such clothing, on her head. The satchels were woven from what appeared to be lutta grass, a grass that was rare around Glendunny. The bandanna looked like something Elsinore might have picked up in a dump-scouring expedition.

"Where's the patient?" the beaver asked.

Patient? The word was unfamiliar to Locksley and Yrynn. "Be patient" was something they had all heard their parents say at one time or another, but patient? What was this?

"Right here." The beavers all backed away from the travois.

"*Incroyable!* Over the falls. Simply incredible," she softly exclaimed as she bent over Dunwattle and pressed her small, flattish ear to his chest. "Heartbeat strong. Good sign. Now stand back." As she spoke, she turned around, squatting and bracing herself with her front legs, then raised her tail and gave Dunwattle's chest a smart smack. Water, pebbles, and river muck, including a smallish trout, were ejected from his mouth.

Another beaver scooted in and picked up the trout, which was still wiggling, and heaved it into the river. Betula readjusted her bandanna slightly, and it was then they saw that she was missing one eye. The bandanna had covered the wrinkled dark pit where her eye had been. Noting their shock, Betula stepped forward.

"Yes, young'uns, I had an unfortunate encounter with a devilish fishhook that had floated downstream. The river gives us many gifts, but not exactly this!" She reached into one of her satchels and held up a large and sharp fishhook. "But I never waste anything. I turned the hook into a tool for my surgery. Thread it with a bit of fish gut and I can sew up any wound. I shall now do just that for the bad cut on your friend's front paw. I had hoped for something just like this hook, for mending the various wounds we often suffer. Some disasters can become a blessing."

"Should we start to move him now, Betula?"

"Not until I sew him up and put on the birch sap," she said, reaching for one of her sacks. With her paw, she took out a glob of what smelled like birch sap but was much thicker. She began to smear it on the worst of Dunwattle's wounds. "This will numb the pain while I stitch."

"Need some more, Betula?" a young beaver just about the age of the kits asked.

"Yes, a bit more."

"Is her name Betula, or is betula her medicine?" Locksley whispered.

The beaver must have overheard them, for she paused and fixed the two beavers in a steely gaze with her single eye.

"I am the Betula. I know the secrets of birch water and I have developed its healing sciences. Hence, I am called the Betula. But when you address me, you may drop the 'the' and simply call me Betula. And for my most intimate friends, well, they call me Betty."

"But of course," Yrynn said.

Betula worked diligently and soon the worst of the wounds were sewn up. After several more applications of betula, the bleeding stopped. Dunwattle was declared ready to be moved. "Draggers begin," Betula ordered. "But mind you, keep a steady pace, not too fast. Not too slow."

They wound their way through woods thick with birch and pine and a scattering of aspen trees. Within a short time, they smelled a pond.

"All right," Betula said. "Direct to the infirmary. Top entry."

Locksley and Yrynn had been wondering how they would carry poor Dunwattle to a lodge. But now they watched in wonder as the beavers began to float the travois on the pond. The pond itself was much smaller than the one of Glendunny, but it had its charm. There were thickets of ferns on its banks and a rare plant known as floramorra, or winter bloom, that blossomed pale pink in the time of the Hunger Moons. Of course, since they ate mostly wood, the beavers did not experience the Hunger Moons with the same anguish as other animals.

"Come in, come in, kits." Betula motioned toward a smallish lodge near the edge of this very small pond.

They followed in the wake of the travois and watched as the woven raft was hauled to almost the top of the lodge. Within another few seconds, the roof of the lodge slid to one side.

"Some engineering feat!" Locksley whispered.

But Yrynn didn't hear him. Instead, she was listening carefully as Betula called out instructions. "Doucement, doucement, chérie." Yrynn gasped. Where had she heard those words before? Her mum, her da—Maman . . . Père! The words came back to her as if from a most distant star. A lullaby her maman had sung to her!

Fais dodo, ma p'tite fille
Fais dodo, t'auras du lolo
Mama est en haut
Papa est en bas

Go to sleep, little girl
Go to sleep, you will have your milk
Mama is up lodge
Papa below at the dam

She now remembered her mother saying something about how the beavers of Glendunny did not like the old language of the Canuck beavers. So that was why she would only sing these songs in a very soft voice when she was trying to get Yrynn to sleep. But here at this pond the beavers spoke many of their words in that forbidden language from the past.

"Come in, come in, kits, our friend is waking up," Betula urged.

Entering by the more traditional underwater passage, Yrynn and Locksley crawled into the lodge and followed the interior tunnel to the top, where now Dunwattle lay on a bed of soft fern fronds and moss. The sharp scent of the birch-water sap permeated the air. Dunwattle seemed to be stirring. His second eyelids, the underwater ones, seemed to be fluttering.

"He's coming to," Betula said. "I have some broth that will help bring him around as soon as his eyes fully open." She held a small, hollowed-out maplewood cup beneath Dunwattle's mouth with a cattail reed to sip through. "The birch water stirred in a maplewood cup always does the trick. Now whatever is that on his ankle?"

"My good-luck charm," Dunwattle muttered. "Kindly remove it now!" Those were Dunwattle's first words.

"Un porte-bonheur." Betula almost cackled. "Bad joke!"

"A very bad joke!" Dunwattle huffed, and a bit of slop from the bottom of the river sprayed from his mouth.

"The last of the river water. That should do it!" Betula said.

And it did.

That evening, Dunwattle had recovered enough to be moved into another, larger lodge in the pond. It was the Aquarius's lodge, which could accommodate all of them more comfortably. It seemed quite generous of the Aquarius to offer them this luxury. In fact, it was almost unimaginable that any Aquarius at Glendunny would ever do such a thing.

The pond, they learned, was called Belle d'Eau, which in the language of the Canadian beavers meant "Beautiful Water." The Aquarius was a gentle female called Lily. For Locksley, Yrynn, and Dunwattle there was no disguising their complete shock upon learning that there were other beavers, Canadian beavers no less, in Scotland.

"B-b-b-but . . . but . . . how have you remained a secret?" Locksley asked.

Lily laughed gently. "A secret from you and the rest of Scotland and England."

"Well, yes, that is true. How did we not know you were here?"

"Miraculous? Is that what you are suggesting?" A beaver whom they thought might be Lily's mate chuckled. But then he directed his attention toward Yrynn. "I see you have a Saska tail."

Saska tail! She hadn't heard that word "Saska" since her parents had vanished. She had been told her tail with finely sloping edges was a Saska, named for their ancestors that had come from a territory called Saskatchewan.

"Yes . . . that is what my parents told me. But how come you never came to our pond in Glendunny? Did you know about it?"

"Indeed," Lily said slowly. There was a foreboding tone in her voice. "And that is why we never came."

"Deuxième classe," someone whispered.

Yrynn muttered, "Second class."

"Yes," said the beaver they suspected was Lily's mate. "My name is Myrr. I was chased away by a particularly repulsive beaver, both in mind and appearance." *Snert*, all three kits thought to themselves. "That of course was years ago. I had heard that the beavers of Glendunny were not especially welcoming. It took me a long time to find Belle d'Eau. There were just a few of us then. But one by one they came. Just a few at a time, mind you, and not many." He cast a glance at Yrynn. "Not your family, I guess."

"No, not mine," she said in a quivering voice. Her life might have been a lot easier had she found this place. But then again, she would have never met Locksley and Dunwattle, her best friends. She cast a glance at Dunwattle. "Is . . . is our friend Dunwattle going to be all right? Will he get better?" Dunwattle seemed to be sleeping peacefully now.

"Of course," Betula said. "But he needs rest. You must stay here for a while."

"So why was it that you were coming our way?" Lily the Aquarius asked.

Yrynn and Locksley exchanged a tense glance.

"We came on a mission."

"And what might that be?" Lily asked.

"We seek the eagles of Iolaire."

"For what purpose?" Lily snapped. Her tone had changed entirely. The lodge was suddenly fraught with tension. The air crackled with a weird energy, as if an electrical storm were brewing. They felt that within seconds the sky would fracture and the black of night would peel back to show shards of lightning dancing a jig.

"We hope they will guide us to our swan," Locksley said.

"We're seeking our swan, Elsinore," Yrynn said. Her voice quaked as if she might break into tears any second.

"Then we have something in common," Lily replied.

"We do?" the kits asked all at once.

Even Dunwattle now roused himself partway from the bed of moss and ferns he'd been placed on. "You have lost your swan, too?" His voice was thin and scratchy.

"Not exactly. We have been swan-less forever here. We have never had a swan, but a lovely swan, one whose name we never knew, we think it was her for she often flew over our pond, she delivered an egg." A terrible silence now descended on the lodge. Lily inhaled deeply. "And that egg was stolen." A bitter darkness seemed to crackle in her eyes.

"Stolen!"

"Yes."

"Who stole the egg?"

"We are not sure. But what we have in common is the eagles of Iolaire. The eagles have vowed to find that egg."

They know something more that they are not telling, thought Dunwattle, who sensed this. He was now alert and saw something pass between Lily and her mate. *This is not the whole story.*

CHAPTER 8

Little Feidah

"Just look at her, Lachlan! Look at the progress she's making. The ring on her ankle with the tether doesn't seem to inhibit her that much."

"Naw," Lachlan said. "She's a pro."

They were in a large barn, watching Elsinore flying in and around and straight up into the rafters.

"But I don't think we can untether her until we are sure she is healed, and far away from the attention of my niece Adelaide."

"Well, we're here on Little Feidah, and Adelaide is back on the mainland with her broken drone."

"Thank goodness!" Glencora muttered.

The two old people both looked up at Elsinore as she

swooped through the air of the cavernous barn that sat on the west side of Glencora's rambling farm, with its green fields and pastures. Glencora sighed deeply. There had once been four or five actual farms, or crofts, on the island, but as the owners grew old and left, Glencora bought up the land.

"Do you think Adelaide has given up on tracking her with those drones?" Lachlan asked.

"No idea, really. She wants to find that beaver she saw. She is sure there is a colony someplace far north on the upper Tweed. She's already read too much about the relationship between swans and beavers. So now she's trying to write some article on symbiotic relationships in nature."

"Symbiotic? What does that mean again, Glencora?"

"The relationships between two different species that help each other."

"Kind of like us, Glencora." The old man chuckled.

"My dear!" Glencora burst out. "You and I are not of different species. We're both human."

"But we are beneficial to each other. Let's be honest. You have the money."

"Don't talk about my money. You are my companion as much as my dear late husband ever was. You make me laugh. And together we were spies—you taught me to fly and I'm not sure what I taught you."

"How to decode and encode," Lachlan answered.

"Yes, yes, of course. I keep forgetting. I did teach coding.

And guess what? You wound up better at it than me."

"Rubbish."

At this point Elsinore swooped lower. She needed to hear this part of the conversation.

"I say we go up there now and check," Lachlan said, nodding at a cupola above the hayloft of the barn.

Glencora looked at her watch. "Yes, just about time for them to get active on Shorty."

The cupola was a simple boxlike structure with slatted sides on the roof of the barn with an entrance from the hayloft. There was a small desk that both Glencora and Lachlan hunched over when they turned on a machine of some sort that they called Shorty. It was a kind of radio. Elsinore would follow them up to the cupola, where they had made a soft bed for her.

"Now take yourself a little snooze, dear," Glencora would say softly. Elsinore would only pretend she was sleeping. Her nearly invisible ears buried in feathers were completely attuned. Swans' hearing was vastly superior to two-legs'. They could detect many more tones and harmonic variations than any human being.

Glencora and Lachlan rarely talked to each other as they listened through their earphones, but there were other voices that came through dimly from the machine called Shorty. Its antenna at the top of the cupola picked up those voices. The thing that most humans did not realize about swans was that Elsinore's species might be called mute swans, but they were not precisely mute and far from deaf. When they were in flight, the beating of their wings made a rhythmic humming sound that other swans could often pick up, even a mile away. It served as a channel for communication. And now what Elsinore heard was Glencora once again muttering another ungentle curse. Eventually the two old people descended from the cupola.

"Sleep tight, dearie." Glencora reached down and gently patted the feathers on Elsinore's head. She sighed. "She seems to like it up here in the cupola almost as much as she liked the library back in Skibodeen." Skibodeen was Glencora's estate on the mainland of Scotland.

"She liked that stained-glass window you had there of the swan."

"Are you suggesting she is a bit vain?"

"Not at all." Lachlan took a moment to finish his thought. "Maybe she just missed her own kind." The words that Lachlan MacLean spoke resonated deeply in Elsinore's mind. *My own kind.* She sensed that her sleep might be disturbed, deeply disturbed, that night.

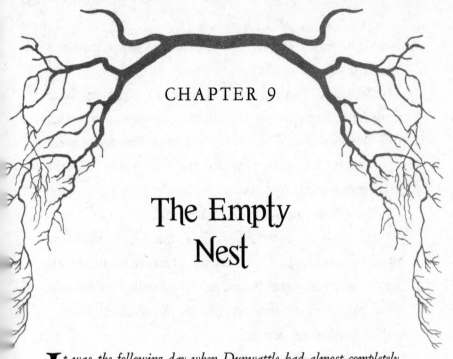

CHAPTER 9

The Empty Nest

It was the following day when Dunwattle had almost completely recovered that they followed the other beavers across the pond to a narrow inlet. Atop a very anonymous-looking lodge, perhaps that of a muskrat, a nest had been built—a swan's nest.

Betula now spoke up. "This is where we found the egg."

"You just found it?" Yrynn asked. "You don't know who brought it?"

"We think it was a swan egg. It was very large," Lily replied.

"And the feather, don't forget the feather," a kit's voice spoke up.

"Yes, indeed, the feather," Lily said softly, nodding at the little kit.

"Was it a bloody feather?" Dunwattle asked, his voice shaking.

"Oh no, not at all," Lily said. "Aryel, go fetch the feather."

The kit climbed into the nest and delicately brought the feather to the beavers.

"Give it to Locksley," Dunwattle said.

Locksley examined it: "Flight feather, remiges—no blood, normal molt. This is usually Elsinore's molting time for secondary remiges." For the beavers of Belle d'Eau, Locksley could have been speaking another language entirely.

"Is it Elsinore's feather?"

"Entirely possible . . . but . . . but we can't be sure."

"But why would she come here?" Dunwattle spoke in a mournful voice. "We're her best friends. Why not bring the egg to us?" Lily extended a paw and stroked Dunwattle's head as if to soothe him. To the kits it was absolutely unimaginable that Elsinore would have an egg. Could care for an egg. Let alone be the mother of an egg. They were her kits, as much as they were the kits of their own parents. It didn't matter that they were not her species. This was something beyond species. Friends . . . best friends! They told Elsinore things they would never dare tell their own parents. Yes, she was a grown-up, but in their minds, she was the perfect grown-up. It mattered not that she was a bird and they were considered rodents, or castors. Species just didn't matter when you were best friends.

Lily continued to speak. "The egg had for some reason been abandoned and she had grieved for it." A hush fell over the kits as they treaded water in the murky light of the pond. Then the last beam of the setting sun seemed to pierce through the brush at the edge of the pond and cast a luminous glow on the empty nest.

"But I still don't understand," Yrynn persisted. "What do we have in common with you and the eagles of Iolaire?"

Lily swam close to Yrynn now and peered deep into her eyes. It gave Yrynn a quiet thrill, for this beaver's fur was burnished just as she must be in this beam of sun, and her eyes were Canadian eyes with a glint of amber in them, unlike those of the Glendunny beavers. These were creatures of her own kind. Lily spoke in a hushed voice, as if addressing only Yrynn, yet Dunwattle and Locksley could hear her. "You seek the eagles to find your swan. We seek the eagles to find our egg."

"But it was the swan who brought this egg to you. Not the eagles," Dunwattle said as he swam closer.

"I told you. We never really saw or met her. She came on a dark and stormy night, and we must have been asleep in our lodge. Though there was work to be done on our dam, it was impossible to transport logs or any material from the Rage."

"The Rage, what's that?" Locksley asked.

"The river, the patch near the falls. That's what we call it this time of year. We didn't even begin to know where to look for such a swan. We are closer with the eagles than to any swan." Now tears streamed from Lily's eyes. "And we are so ashamed that we could not protect the egg. We had all promised together that we could take good care of it. For we knew how important swans can be to beaver ponds. We thought it such a blessing when we found it that first night. And we did take care of it. We tucked fresh thick moss around it every night. Never letting it get damp. The owls of our woods brought us molted feathers to keep the nest dry. See, here's one." Lily reached with her paw and plucked out a downy fringe feather that grew on the edges of some owl's wings to silence their flight. "They are the best for trapping air between the twigs. And meadow grasses, yes, the muskrats brought us that. But we still failed that dear swan." The other beavers began to murmur, each speaking softly as to how they had contributed to this nest.

It seemed to the three young kits that the nest almost began to glow as they spoke. Their love, their adoration, for this egg was palpable. It was as if one could reach out and touch it—except there was no egg now. There was a void in this pond of Belle d'Eau as profound as the void in the kits' hearts. They were all wrapped in the grief of missing something beloved. And yet the egg had not even hatched.

So how could one grieve what had never been there in life? Never hatched. Never lived. All three kits could nonetheless feel the grief of the beavers of this pond deeply.

"How did it happen?" Dunwattle asked. "If you were guarding the egg as you explained, how did it happen? A two-leg?"

"Possibly, but we can't be sure," Myrr, Lily's mate, said. "You see, I was on guard duty that day and it seems that when I dove under just for a second to check the foundations of the muskrat nest . . . well, there was a thin current of water that carried an odd smell. I think that I actually fell asleep, but for maybe only two seconds. The same thing happened with Olly except he was above water. We both went to sleep, but for just a second, and when we woke the egg was gone. But later we did find something in the nest, and then something similar in the water."

"What was that?" Yrynn asked.

"It was bright blue and about the size of a pebble. It seemed half melted, but there was some sand or white grit in it."

"Blue pebbles but no tracks?" Locksley asked.

"No tracks at all. Lynx have been known to steal bird eggs, but they eat them right on the spot. You can find the broken shells afterward. But there were no broken shells. Nothing. Not a trace. Only these strange blue pebbles," Myrr said. "And yet . . ." The beaver's voice dropped off.

"And yet what?" Dunwattle asked.

"I feel now that the moment it was seized, even in my sleep, I sensed something was amiss. Not quite right."

"And so, the eagles of Iolaire are going to help you?" Lily and Myrr both nodded.

"And we too have been told to seek them out to help us find our swan," Locksley said. Locksley now swam closer to Lily. "Do you think that the swan who brought you this egg knows it has been stolen?"

Betula now surfaced nearby. "Well, as you heard Myrr say, he himself had a crinkle in his skeat. Yet swans don't have skeats, so that swan might not know."

"But," Dunwattle said, "they have *schwanka*."

"Schwanka?" all the beavers whispered to one another. *Of course*, thought Dunwattle. They would not have known of schwanka, since they never had a pond swan. He turned back to Locksley. "Locksley, explain to them about schwanka and the head feathers. Locksley is an expert on swan feathers."

"Well," Locksley began, "schwanka is a special sleep state in which higher thinking can occur." He continued with a brief explanation about how the tiny sensitive feathers clustered around a swan's head gave the swan a unique ability to think as she slept. "Twenty-five thousand feathers in a cluster around their skulls, 'warming' their brains, which allows for a kind of superior dream state during which they are most sensitive."

The beavers seemed suitably impressed and whispered among themselves.

"So," Dunwattle said, "if she were dreaming, the swan who brought you the egg just might know that the egg has been stolen and where it might be." A thrill of excitement seemed to pass through the beavers of the Belle d'Eau pond.

"Really?" Lily the Aquarius stepped forward. Her rich brown eyes glistened with hope.

"Well, possibly," Locksley said. He didn't want to get their hopes up too much. And what if Elsinore was dead? *Live, Elsinore, please! Live!*

And indeed, in the cupola of a barn on the island of Little Feidah, a swan slumbered in deepest schwanka. The twenty-five thousand feathers clustered around her head began to tremble. She was dreaming of Wyntersphree. And then words of Lachlan MacLean came back to her in her sleep. *Maybe she just missed her own kind.*

When Elsinore had heard those few words, her heart skipped a beat. Sometimes two-legs really did surprise her. She truly had missed her own kind, and that was what had led her to go back to Eyja Svane, the island of the swans far to the north, in the sea of Wyntersphree. This was where she had found the abandoned nest with the egg. Now in deep schwanka, she recalled specifically why she had made that brief trip just a month before she had been so grievously wounded by the lynx. It was not simply missing her own kind. Something had called to her then. Though vague, it seemed to be a kind of yearning that filtered into her sleep and then lingered during her waking hours in Glendunny. So, she had left Glendunny, and as she drew closer to the sea of Wyntersphree and the island of Eyja Svane, she realized that she was grieving for something lost or dead. A cygnet? She knew, knew deep in her head feathers, where swans often had their most profound thoughts, that this was what mourning felt like.

The first moments when grief besieged her, she thought, *Why me—of all swans?* Mateless, cygnet-less, never having laid an egg, how could this be happening? But the very second she had spotted that egg in the abandoned nest, her grief and her yearning had been put to rest. She knew precisely what she would do. Spreading her three front toes, she plucked the egg from the abandoned nest and clutched it in the leathery pocket of the webbing of her feet, her "lomme," as it was called. She then flew the egg to the beavers of Belle d'Eau, the Canucks! She had only discovered these beavers two moons before. She had been shocked at the time with this discovery and had sworn she would not divulge their whereabouts to anyone—especially the beavers of Glendunny, who had a deep prejudice against

Canadian beavers. The Glendunny beavers' history and prejudice against Canuck castors was not something to be proud of. But she was proud of Dunwattle and Locksley, who had accepted Yrynn, a Canuck herself, so readily and with friendship.

But now, in the midst of deep schwanka, she knew that something had happened to that egg she had delivered to the beavers of Belle d'Eau. The dream obsessed her. An evil act had occurred, and she must right that wrong. Elsinore was driven to return to Wyntersphree. She must go to the old nest in which the egg had been abandoned. She must retrace her wingbeats from there to Belle d'Eau. In order to make sense of this grief, she had to go back before she could go forward. It was as if the egg had not been abandoned this time. But something else. Something worse had happened to that egg.

"Stalt kyll," she muttered, and woke up. Stolen! That was it. In the language of Old Swan, stalt kyll meant that an egg with a chick had been stolen. And now Elsinore knew that this was true. Besieged by this new misery, she immediately began to gnaw the ring from her ankle. It did not take her long to free herself. Once unshackled, she squeezed between the slatted windows of the cupola and launched herself into flight on that beckoning, familiar wind from the north. She turned her head once and looked back. *Vertu-zel y Ha det,*

she thought. It was the swan blessing for soul spirits. And Elsinore knew that Glencora and Lachlan were her human soul spirits.

The breezes soon billowed beneath her wings, and she felt their crisp edge as she angled her flight feathers. The fine fluffles, as her head feathers were called, seemed to thrill to the salt breeze. Her mind had never felt sharper. *Thank you, Lachlan*, she thought. For she was deeply grateful to the old man who had mended her injuries with his stiff but gentle fingers. Her feathers were working beautifully now, and she began to soar into the clear blue of the morning sky.

Within hours she was flying up the fjord of the Wyntersphree sea where she had been born, toward the island of Eyja Svane, the source of her original grief—that abandoned egg she had found in a nest not more than a league from her own birthplace.

PART TWO

New Eden

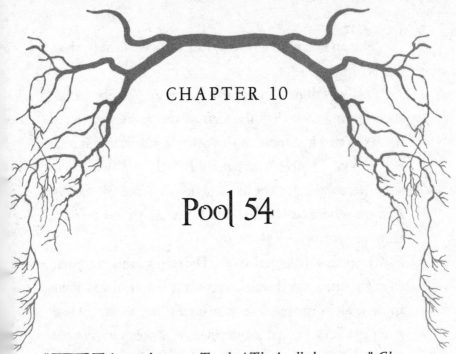

CHAPTER 10

Pool 54

"We're together, pups. Together! That's all that counts," Glory said softly.

But Edlmyn and Iglemore found little comfort in their mum's words. They had grown accustomed to the watery rustle of the ocean that varied according to the winds. The pool was very different from the sea or river. There was no current. It was unnaturally still and yet there was a constant thrumming. Sometimes there were roaring sounds that seemed not borne of wind or water but rather originating from some unnatural, strange source. But of course, this entire place was unnatural. They were not outside, so where exactly were they?

"Not a river," Iglemore had said.

"Not an ocean," their mum had whispered softly, shaking her head.

The Not, Edlmyn thought. *We are in the Not.* She looked about, trying to review the strange things she saw. She'd heard the two-legs speak of this place in which they'd been put as pool 54, and it was peculiar. The pool was circular, perfectly circular, not like a pond—not like Glendunny. And the water was not fresh like Glendunny but a bit salty. However, not as salty as the sea.

The otter Edy looked about. The sides of this pool were mostly transparent. It wasn't very deep, but she dived down anyway. She discovered certain places like springs where water did flow in, and some where it flowed out. But the most interesting feature that she discovered was that their pool was in some way connected with other water sources. It was like a maze. Yet there was no passage from the pool occupied by the otters that had any connection to these other waterways. Nevertheless, Edy sensed signs of life around them, if not in their own pool. She dived under again. Then, holding her breath as long as she could, she opened her eyes. Were they all alone? Were there any other creatures in this peculiar place?

Occasionally, Edy heard a loud two-leg voice reverberate through the space. That was all she could call it—a space. There was no sky. No trees. No riverbanks or land of any sort. Not a star. Not a moon. This was a place of complete and total nothingness. Then the otters gasped as they saw a beautiful shade of pink and a flow of bubbles in the channel outside of their pool.

"What's that?" Edy gasped as she turned her head and saw what appeared to be a long streaming cloud that had filtered into the nothingness. Then soft bubbles rose in the water above the pink streak. They realized that they were much like the bubbles they had seen in the Across before they were captured.

"It's a dolphin—a pink dolphin, Mum!" She hesitated. "I thought dolphins were only gray."

A voice softly reverberated from the channel. "Not all of us! Think again. Indeed, I am a dolphin! But not from the sea where you came from. I come from a very distant river. I am Pink."

"Most certainly!" Glory said.

"Pink is what I am called here, but my species name is *Inia geoffrensis*. And in some countries, my cousin dolphins are considered sacred. But not here. Not in New Eden." She sighed and a stream of little bubbles rose in the water. "Nothing is sacred here. Here I am valued because I am shaped like a torpedo."

"Torpedo?"

"Have you never heard of a torpedo? Of course not! It's an underwater missile perfectly designed for destruction."

"Why?" Glory asked. "Destroy what?"

"Whatever the two-legs please." She sighed wearily.

"But how do you destroy things?"

"They strap bombs to me, explosives. When I reach the target zone, they push a button and the missiles fire with the bombs."

"But why aren't you killed?" Glory asked. She could not believe that she was having this conversation in front of her pups.

"Sometimes we are. So far, I have survived. But many of my mates have not. . . ." Her voice dwindled. "Sorry, must go now, a guard is coming soon. I'll be back. But wait—before I leave, I'll show you something fun. I'll give you a quick bubble show."

"A bubble show?"

"Yes, here's some puffy clouds for you." They heard a few soft snorts and within seconds three batches of puffy clouds were floating above Pink's head. "They call them cumulus clouds. And now your basic cirrus clouds."

"Oh, they look like feathers!" Edy burst out.

"A bit of a magician, I am," she said as she swam off. But the remark was not lost on the pups.

"What's a magician, Mum?" Iggy asked.

"I think it's what we need to get out of here."

"Is Pink a magician?"

"Maybe. Let's hope."

Now, as Glory surfaced, the voices filled this dark and peculiar maze of water. "Adjust salinity on watercourse two A, release orca fourteen and the big blues, X and Y."

Orca. Glory thought she remembered her mum saying something about orcas, but she had no idea what they were. She suddenly was aware of a huge dark shadow gliding by, in a deep channel on the other side of their own transparent barrier. But soon there were puddles of whiteness in the dark. "By my stars!" Glory said in wonder as she swam close to her daughter, Edy. "I believe . . ." She hesitated because this strange pattern of black and white continued to flow by them. "I believe that is indeed an orca."

"A what?" Edy asked.

"A killer whale."

"A killer!"

"Worse than the great white shark?" Iggy whispered.

"Well, maybe, I don't really know. Just heard about them. Remember we're river otters."

"But Mum, do you think that you might know this from the time of the mustah?"

"The mustah was millions and millions of years ago. And I am definitely not that old, dear!"

"I know, but you said yourself . . . things have been coming back to you from that time when all the species of otters were one. When there were no divisions between rivers and seas. The time of the All Water."

Glory sighed. "Yes, I do have a few instincts, I think, mustah instincts."

"Huh?" both pups said at once.

"What exactly are instincts?" Edy asked.

"Instincts are kind of like hunches. They are with you from the time you are born and in some strange way link you back to the deep past of your species in the time of what we call the mustah. It's almost as if as you grow older, you grow younger and can perceive a glimmering of what you once were when your kind first began. You come full circle, as it were. . . .

"Yes, yes . . . ," Glory said softly to herself as she thought of that time of the All Water, where some of her ancestral memories lingered.

The orca seemed to slow down a bit and pause by the window where Iglemore had joined his sister and mother. They pressed their faces against the glass. The orca rolled a bit.

"Where's his eye?" Iggy asked. "I don't see it."

"How do you know it's a 'he'?" Edy asked. "Could be a 'she.'"

"Well, whether the orca is a he or a she, I still don't see any eyes."

"There it is!" their mum interrupted. "You see that splash of white on its head? My word, it's almost the shape of the Glendunny pond," Glory exclaimed. "Now look toward the corner. The eye is in the black part, not the white. And it's absolutely black—black on black."

"Do you think it sees us?" Iggy asked.

"She," a voice came through the glass.

"Holy Lontra!" Iggy exclaimed.

"Iggy, do not take the name of First Otter in vain!"

"But Mum, he spoke—" There was a strange watery growl that emanated from the orca. "I mean 'she,'" Iggy immediately corrected.

"Move along, number fourteen," a voice from a walkway above resonated. A long stick with some sort of hook on the end prodded the orca.

"Atta girl," the voice said. "Treat waiting for you at station Liberty."

The otters saw a female two-leg who grasped a pole.

"Look at her claws. Bright red!" Iggy whispered, and blinked.

"I think they call them fingers," Edy replied.

Liberty, thought the orca named Hvala. *They wouldn't know Liberty if it smacked them in their stupid faces.* But she kept these thoughts to herself and swam on to station Liberty, where a human female leaned over the edge of a projecting platform, holding a mackerel in her hand.

"Open wide, sweetie. You beautiful orca!"

Hvala opened her mouth—all fifty-four of her teeth

flashed. These teeth were spaced perfectly for grabbing prey, which was exactly what she did and then swam away. Delicately, she bit down on the fish. This was a cautionary measure before actually chewing and swallowing. Her back teeth struck the capsule immediately. *All righty*, she thought, *if that's what you're doing, I can play that game too. Let me do a course correction here.*

She now swam to the deepest part of the channel and took a dive to the very bottom, where a series of outflow vents was arranged. She pressed her mouth to the duct and the capsule was sucked right out while she clamped her tongue to the top of her mouth so the mackerel would not go with it. It was a complicated maneuver, but she had mastered it. And so had the other creatures who were imprisoned in this place of darkness that was neither land nor sea, sky nor earth, or as Edy had dubbed it—the Not.

Time to pay a visit to Blekka, Hvala the orca thought.

CHAPTER 11

Blekka

One never knew what state one might find Blekka in. The octopus lived in the deepest part of the central channel of New Eden, but some distance from the array of outlet vents. She normally resided in a pile of concrete blocks that the humans had arranged beneath a rocky outcrop. It had been designed and constructed by two-legs the creatures in New Eden called the Shadows. The sources of light in this freakish place were scant, and the figures of the two-legs who crossed the myriad walkways to feed and attend the imprisoned animals appeared mostly as shadows in the eyes of their prisoners. They were a species apart from any two-legs they had ever encountered or heard about.

Hvala reached the shelf. It was often a bit of a guess as to which of many states she would find her best friend, Blekka, in. And she was always anxious. Now the orca found her friend tied up in a clump of knots of her own eight arms. This was a common sleeping posture for octopuses. The only clue to Blekka's mood was her color. If she was simply sleeping, her color would be bone white or perhaps grayish, but if she was dreaming, she could begin to change. Hvala waited, then sighed as she saw a faint blush rising through the gray. Within a split second there was a mesmerizing shift of color as Blekka began to dream. First pink, then red, then a deep purple blending to green. The colors suffused her body in slow, almost rhythmic succession. It was as mysterious as the shifting lights in the northern sky that came in midsummer—the ones the creatures at the top of the world called the Northern Lights.

Octopuses are such peculiar creatures, Hvala thought every time she approached one. With their eight arms and three hearts tucked away in various parts of their sprawling body, what could be more curious? And the mouth itself was located where one would least expect. Not on its face or head but folded at the center point of its body where the eight arms met. And not only did it not look like a mouth, but it seemed to have the appearance of a beak—like a bird; but most extraordinary of all was that Blekka, like all octopuses, had a single brain. Yet that brain was spread out, distributed through the eight tentacles or arms of the octopus. It was through the arms that information was processed and interpreted. Details concerning depths, or currents, or prey, directed the instincts and behavior of the octopus and guided the creature through the water for food or shelter or alerted it to danger.

Hvala continued to watch as Blekka dreamed. What distant sea was she now recalling? She studied Blekka for long moments while the creature slept. One of Blekka's eyes was quite a bit larger than the other. And although she slept, that eye was open. Its pupil had narrowed to a horizontal slit.

What did she dream about with that large eye? *Freedom?* Yes, most likely. But with octopuses, freedom was a complicated thing. Birth and death were linked in a peculiar way. For a female octopus giving birth, laying eggs was a slow undertaking, entangled with death. Hvala knew that although Blekka had never laid any eggs she dreamed of doing so almost ceaselessly. Eggs were Blekka's grip on eternity. But not here. She had vowed she would never release eggs in this hell of New Eden. She must be free, and this was because for an octopus laying eggs was also the first step toward death. She vowed that she would not die in New Eden.

Although Blekka was driven to reproduce, that very act would kill her. When the time came for her first clutch of eggs to hatch, the female octopus would begin to starve herself. She would even tear at her own body until it became shreds, perhaps thinking that her own flesh would somehow nourish those infant octopuses and even the eggs that were still unhatched. She would tend the offspring faithfully for months, wafting currents of water over the newly hatched so they could catch the nutrients of the sea. She would even stir the water delicately around the waiting strands of eggs that hung like threads of teardrops from a rocky shelter deep in the ocean. The octopus had a name for this care that she gave so lavishly at her own expense. The word was *forn*, or sacrifice. *Fornykho*, which meant ultimate sacrifice.

Would Hvala ever know if Blekka had egg sacs tucked away somewhere beneath the concrete shelf? She knew that Blekka would not want her young to hatch in this shadowy place of evil. However, Hvala would never know if there were eggs or not, as Blekka was an expert at hiding things away. And although she was large and could stretch so long, she could still pour herself into the tiniest chinks and cracks—perfect, perhaps, for laying eggs. Blekka didn't precisely swim; she flowed, she oozed. In Hvala's eyes, she was almost mystical and Blekka was her best friend.

Now, as a soft iridescent violet covered the skin of Blekka, Hvala sensed she was awakening.

The large eye blinked.

"So?" Two of her arms swelled slightly, as if the mouth beneath them, in what humans would call an armpit, had opened wide to yawn. Hvala thought for the thousandth time how confusing it could be to really understand an octopus. Its anatomy was completely and totally insane. Nothing was where it should be.

Blekka was totally alert now. "I take it you came here to ask about those newly captured otters?" Often Hvala felt that Blekka was almost a mind reader.

"Well, the littlest one, the female—they call her Edy. She seems quite bright. They all do, actually, but she's the most curious."

"Hmmm . . . have they been fed yet?"

"Yes. But no sign of sluggishness so far."

"In other words, I have to get to work."

"Yes. I'm afraid so. Up to pouring tonight?" "Pouring" was the word that Hvala called Blekka's expeditions.

"I suppose I should get to it before they have digested the capsules. I'll go now before dawn. We don't want those capsules dissolving in their guts. Must keep them alert. Train the otters how to pick them out before swallowing. Dawn is coming on. I better get on with it. Most digestion in mammals occurs before dawn."

"Dawn," Hvala murmured. How any creature would know what time it was in this dark and timeless place defied imagination. Somehow, Blekka with her strange body and incredible brain could recognize things that other creatures could not. Octopuses were like swimming libraries of information.

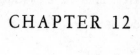

CHAPTER 12

Venting
and Vomiting

T he otters were unsure how long they had been in pool 54, but they soon heard an odd popping sound. Looking toward the rim of the pool, they saw something most peculiar. Was it a large worm or a snake? Or was it several snakes and worms entangled with one another? Each time it moved, there was a *pock pock* sound. It slipped into the water now. The creature began moving slowly, flowing with its arms unfurling, then coiling, twirling, and stretching yet never ceasing to move. One large eye seemed to fix on them.

"Have you eaten?"

"Who are you?" Glory asked.

"Have you eaten?" Blekka repeated the question.

"Yes, yes. We have. They gave us mussels and clams, but out of the shell. Very strange."

"Of course!" Blekka said.

"Most unnatural," Glory replied.

"Not if they wanted to poison you."

"Poison!" Glory gasped.

"Of course. Well, not quite poison your body, but your mind."

"Whyever would they do that? What in Lontra would we do with poisoned minds?" The pups opened their eyes wide with alarm. Their mum rarely swore using the name of First Otter.

"It's their bidding you would do, madame." A stream of bubbles flushed from the creature as one arm unfurled. A small blue capsule was revealed in the first of several suction cups on that arm.

"This, my friends, is the poison. You have already swallowed it, most likely." Blekka sighed. "As you said, they fed you clams, mussels without their shells."

"Yes." Glory nodded. "We found it odd."

"Permit me to explain," Blekka said. "The capsule was buried in the flesh of the clam. The Shadows had inserted it there. Had they left it in the shell, it would have dropped out before you took your first bite of that clam. But now that blue capsule is in your stomach."

"Oh dear!" Glory wailed, and the two pups began to whimper.

"No . . . no . . . Mum, we don't want to die. We don't want to die."

"Pull yourself together!" Blekka said sharply. Although she could hardly serve as a good example of pulling oneself together, as it seemed to the otters she was oozing all over the place. They simply could not focus on her head, where that one big eye was lodged next to a much smaller second eye. "Now follow me and I shall give you your first lesson in venting."

"Venting?" the pups said. "What's that?"

"You'll see soon enough," Blekka replied.

Glory and her pups swam behind Blekka in her flowing wake to the far side of the pool. They watched as she wrapped four of her eight arms around the edges of a disk. Within seconds she had pried it loose. They felt a strong current flowing as water was sucked from the pool through what Blekka had called the vent.

"Now when I count to three, I want your mother to press her mouth to this vent and let it suction up all that you have eaten."

"You want us to throw up?" Edy said.

"It won't hurt, believe me."

Iggy sneered. "It'll just feel as if our guts are being pulled out. That's all."

"No arguments!" Glory barked at her pups. "Do what the creature says." She looked at Blekka, trying to figure out what exactly she was—fish? Worm? Sea snake? Perhaps if they had spent a longer time at sea on the Across, they might have encountered a sea animal like her. But they had not.

The pups trembled with fear as their mum approached the vent and pressed her mouth to it as Blekka had ordered. They saw her stomach convulse. And then what sounded like a large belch.

"Mum . . . Mum. Are you all right?"

Glory turned to her pups. "Actually, pups . . . I . . . I feel fine."

"All right, you're next," Blekka said, nodding at Iglemore.

Iggy pressed his mouth to the vent. There was another large belch. "I . . . I'm all right." He blinked as if surprised that he had not been turned completely inside out. Edy followed. Her body seemed to jerk a bit, but she did it and back paddled from the vent.

"Good!" Blekka said, releasing a stream of happy bubbles. "Now just let me put the cover back on the vent."

Then she gave the otters a quick lesson in how to search for the blue capsules in their food and to remove them before eating.

"When you find the blue capsules, take them to the vent and that will flush them away. You otters have fine motor skills. You're very handy, as two-legs would say. And like two-legs you have opposable thumbs. Excellent for manipulating small objects."

"Yes, but what is this all about? Why are they trying to poison us? Why are we here? Is it forever?" Glory asked, her voice full of anguish.

"We are here, captured for the dark purposes of the Shadow people," Blekka replied. "But we are dedicated to revolution, to escaping. To finding our freedom in the world where we were born and where we belong. Our destiny has been robbed. We have become tools of evil. A poem I once heard a two-leg recite says it best. It is a call to defend the earth and all its seas for the freedom of all those who inhabit earth. The poem is ancient, but the thoughts should never die."

And now a shimmering radiance began to spread through Blekka as she recited the words of the poem "The Garden" by Andrew Marvell. As the words flowed from her, she was becoming a glittering constellation in the murkiness of this dark place.

The mind, that ocean where each kind
Does straight its own resemblance find,
Yet it creates, transcending these,
Far other worlds, and other seas.
Annihilating all that's made
To a green thought in a green shade.

Blekka sighed. "That is our destiny, my friends, to make the ocean we live in green, to make a green shade where all can grow and live."

"But how?" Glory asked. "How can we find freedom? How can we escape?"

"The time will come. When we are ready, you will see. But in the meantime, we must keep our minds alert. The blue capsules that these Shadows put in our food are meant to dull our brains. We spit them out. We must keep our minds alive. Do you know that there are creatures here who have never seen the light of day or the stars of the night? They were born here. Their eggs were brought here before they hatched. Mothers have given birth here after they were captured."

"So, what do you do to keep the dream of freedom alive? For freedom must be just a dream for creatures who have never seen the light of a real day or the green of an ocean."

Blekka spoke more slowly, as if she were thinking deeply. "I know you are confused by not only what I have told you, but about me and what kind of creature I am. Well, I am a mollusk. There are many fancy scientific names to describe my species, but I'll stop at mollusk and tell you that I am a most peculiar animal with my eight arms, three hearts, and my very strange brain—a single brain that spreads out through my body. I can think through not just my head but my tentacles, my eight arms. Within this hodgepodge of a body, I hold the stories that creatures live for. That give them a passion for freedom. I tell them how the moon rises and what it looks like in all its phases." Blekka's body turned a dusky dark like twilight, as luminous blotches began to float across her skin. Around her eyes a starburst pattern suddenly blossomed.

"I tell them about breaking dawns and blazing sunsets." Colors of pink, then glowing oranges and fiery reds began to slide across her skin. The otters looked in wonder. They had seen sunsets and dawns like that, but not in this way. Not embodied by a living creature. In those days at sea as they swam the Across toward Canada, there was nothing more splendid than the sun splashing down in the west and painting the horizon at day's end. "This is what I do," Blekka said. "I am the storyteller."

The little otter family watched as the octopus flowed back to the side of the pool. Then, slapping her arms onto the transparent walls, she began to slide up to the walkway. There was the *pock pock* sound as her suckers gained their grip on the walls of the pool, then released when she moved up. Her color had changed again, and she was now almost as transparent as the walls she climbed, but then something very curious began to occur. Glory had climbed onto a rock in the center of the pool where she had a good view of the walkway. The walkway itself was metal, but more of a grate with very small spaces in between. Suddenly within a matter of two seconds Blekka's color seemed to change again. It was as if she were becoming the grate. The pattern on her skin was in fact a precise replica of that metal walkway. How did she do this? One minute she had become as transparent as the walls of the pool she was climbing, and the next she had become part of the grate of the walkway.

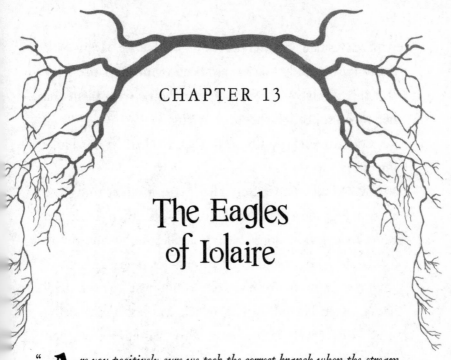

CHAPTER 13

The Eagles of Iolaire

"**A**re you positively sure we took the correct branch when the stream split around that rock?" Dunwattle asked. He was now fully recovered.

"Yes," said Yrynn, although there was a slight quiver in her voice. "This is the way Lily, the Aquarius, directed us."

"I know you, Yrynn. I know that warble in your voice. You're having doubts."

"Dunwattle, there is nothing wrong with having doubts. Look, if you know so much, why don't you lead?"

"Will you two shut up?!" Locksley almost roared. "I'm sick and tired of your squabbling."

"We're not squabbling!" Yrynn said.

"Yes, we are, Yrynn. Yes . . . yes . . . we are." Dunwattle began to stammer. "You've j-just been weird ever since w-we met those beavers. I think you want to be with them and not with us. Because they're your kind."

Locksley and Yrynn both gasped. Then Yrynn broke into tears.

"My kind!" she wailed. "That is the meanest thing you ever said to me. My kind. You are worse than Tonk and Retta and all those horrid beavers at Glendunny who always looked down on me and my parents for being Canucks. I am a beaver, no matter the color of my pelt!" Yrynn drew herself up to her full height, which was not much, seeing as all beavers were rather squat. They had never seen their friend so angry. Dunwattle was about to apologize. But suddenly there was a fierce gust of wind. Shadows enclosed them and there was a loud beating of wings. Dunwattle screamed. Yrynn and Locksley froze as they saw Dunwattle's feet and tail rising above the water of the stream into midair. The silhouettes of two immense wings spread over the surface of the water.

"Great Castor," Locksley began to swear, but then felt himself rising as something pinched through his fur. The stream babbled beneath Locksley. Out of the corner of his eye, he saw Yrynn dangling like himself.

Slowly Yrynn began to speak, enunciating each word,

each syllable. "We . . . have . . . found . . . the eagles . . . Dunwattle."

"Or maybe they found us," Dunwattle replied. He looked down as the earth receded. They were by this time higher than the tallest trees. He felt a serious queasiness in his skeat. *Don't throw up . . . don't throw up . . .* How embarrassing to throw up in front of Yrynn, because secretly Dunwattle was in love with Yrynn, despite his furious accusations a minute before. Although he was always too shy to actually profess his love for Yrynn. He had written poems about her but never given them to her. But it was going to be very hard to ever write another love poem if he'd thrown up in front of her, or worse, on her. For at this moment, the eagle with Yrynn was flying below him. "Oh Castor," Dunwattle prayed, "don't let me upple kukkle. Puleeeze, I'll do anything not to upple."

"Dunwattle!" Yrynn cried. "Open your eyes. This is incredible."

"I can't, I might . . . I might . . ."

"Upple?" Yrynn's voice threaded through the drafts of air.

A rough voice cut the air just above Dunwattle's head.

"Never before has anyone uppled on me in all my years of flying, which I can assure you are many."

"Forgive me," Dunwattle replied in a small voice. "I

didn't mean to insult you. I would never insult your kind."

"And what kind do you think I am?"

"Eagle, perhaps?"

"Yes." The voice was slow. "Largest eagles on earth. Now open your eyes, boy, and take in the view."

Boy? all three beavers thought. *What's a boy?*

Then Yrynn recalled her lessons from Two-legs Vigilance class. "That's a two-leg word, isn't it? For young males?"

"Precisely," the eagle answered.

"B-b-b-but . . . ," Locksley, who was being carried by another eagle, stammered. "And the name for young females is 'girl'?"

"Right-o, sonny."

Boy, girl . . . All the words two-legs used to describe young two-legged human children flooded through the three kits' minds. They had learned all this in Two-legs Vigilance class with Castor Helfenbunn. They each vividly remembered the lodge where TLV was taught. It had a poster with the words "KNOW THY ENEMY." There were pictures of all sorts of two-legs on it. Grown-up men and women, children, even one with the queen of England and the ancient and most dreadful king Henry VIII. The vicious monarch who not only beheaded two of his six wives, but craved beaver fur and was said to love boiled or fried beaver tail. The gruesome monarch took it any way he could get it. "Such a charming fellow!" as Miss Kukla, the librarian at Glendunny, would say with a smirk on her slightly grizzled face.

"But stop fussing about words," the eagle who was carrying Dunwattle scolded. "Open up your eyes, all of you, and take in the view." Yrynn had already opened her eyes as night had fallen. The constellations were just rising and began assembling themselves into configurations—the Great Castor, the lynx, the swan, the wolf, the muskrat, and the otter—all the creatures of the ponds and the forests of the beaver world.

She was scanning the starry sky for Stellamara, or Little Blue, as she used to call the wolf cub star. She often thought of them as her star friends. She knew their stories from the tales her own mum had told her. The night was not yet dark enough for the wolf cub star to be glimpsed, but as the world unfolded beneath them, Dunwattle finally dared to open his eyes.

It was in fact beautiful as dusk crept across the land. To the west where the sun was setting, on what appeared to be an endless sea, low clouds smoldered red on the horizon. To the east the night was turning a deep lavender and the first stars were teetering shyly on the rim of another endless sea. A scattering of small dusky islands floated magically beneath him. Dunwattle could not believe quite how much he was seeing. How much he had missed from spending most of his short lifetime in the tight circle of Glendunny pond. Once he thought that pond was so huge. He thought the whole world was Glendunny until that fateful night when he was scared by a ghost. Fleeing madly from the ghost of Lorna, he swam to Dam 8 in the minutes before the dawn. He then climbed over the dam and plunged into a stream that led to the Tweed River. Hours later he committed the gravest of all sins of the beaver community, vysculf—that of being seen by a two-leg.

But now, clutched in the talons of an enormous eagle, he realized he had never felt freer. It was as if he had slipped the skin of the earth. That was how Elsinore had described flying. Except for the somewhat rackety noise of the wind through the eagle's huge wings, it all seemed silent. The stars were now rising like shoals in the night.

Dunwattle felt a change in the air pressure. The eagle was slowing his flight and they were carving a turn in the sky.

"Wind south by southwest." It was the voice of the eagle who was carrying Yrynn. "Two points off of Venus, then course correction for landing upwind."

"Venus!" Yrynn whispered. *Very old school,* Mistress Kukla would say. She often called two-leg words or expressions "old school," which meant that they dated back to a previous era. The names of the stars and the constellations, she had explained, were in Latin or Greek—very old two-leg languages. Beavers did not use Latin or Greek. They named the stars after their world. Stars and constellations were named for the creatures of Glendunny—the lynx constellation or the Big Muskrat, which came in early spring, or the Great Castor. Yrynn was immersing herself in the vast expanse of the starscape over her head. She scanned the sky for Stellamara or Little Blue, but he had not risen yet.

"Weather coming in from the east, better head for Big Nest," the eagle carrying Locksley reported. In that same instant, there was a sharp crack as lightning crashed on the darkened sea. Then a thunderous quake shook the air. The three kits began to tremble. They had never in their lives been out in a thunderstorm. They would always dive deep into the pond, then surface in their weathertight lodges. Occasionally, there might be just a flash of a sliver of lightning glimpsed through the wattling, the woven branches of the roofs of their lodges.

The air now became rougher. The eagles' talons gripped them tighter. Soon they were flying through a pelting rain over a storm-tossed sea, with veins of lightning fracturing the night. *Bones!* That was all that Dunwattle could think of, bones like those of Lorna, his ghost friend who had appeared to him that night and that now seemed years ago. Those bones had driven him out of his lodge in fear. But later, once he had gotten to know Lorna, they had become fast friends. *Lorna*, he thought, *where are you now?*

Then, out of the splintered sky, amid the clamor of the storm there came a voice, a familiar voice with the brogue of the Highlands.

Neamorra, Dunwattle ... Neamorra ...

CHAPTER 14

The Big Nest

But all Dunwattle could think was, *Yeah, Lorna, Neamorra, your heaven. But I just might be heading for my hell.* The eagles had settled down by this time, in a huge nest. Never could the kits have imagined such a nest. It was as large as three or maybe four beaver lodges. Certainly as big as the lodge of their leader, the Castor Aquarius. The nest was at the top of an oak tree that groaned and swayed a bit in the wind. The kits counted six eagles perched on the edge of the nest. This meant twelve eyes with penetrating gazes as sharp as the shards of the lightning that crackled overhead. Was there a light in those eagles' eyes? One of curiosity? Fear? Disdain? The kits couldn't tell. Finally, one spoke. It was a voice very different in tone from the caw or the high piping sound of most birds of prey. This voice was deep and vibrant yet at the same time hushed.

"What brings you here?" An eagle extended his head toward Yrynn. It was as if she had accidentally stepped into the crosshairs of his sights—as though she were a fish about to be snatched from the sea or a rabbit scurrying through a meadow. *I am prey!* Yrynn thought. The eagle repeated his question. "What brings you here?"

It wasn't a time to argue, but she was tempted to say, *Well, actually, sir, the eagles brought us here. Scooped us up and flew right off.* But she didn't. Instead, she swallowed and spoke softly.

"A feather," Yrynn replied.

"A feather and not an egg?"

"Yes, an egg as well," Yrynn said.

And now this eagle stretched out his neck very far. His breath was hideously smelly—the breath of a carrion eater. Like the stink of lynx breath, which could be overwhelming. Poor Dunwattle thought he might upple again. *Oh, just for a whiff of turtle breath. Clean green mossy turtle breath.* "But we don't lay eggs." He gagged as he said the words.

"You take us for stupid?" The eagle's eyes seemed to shoot fire.

Dunwattle gasped. "Oh never . . . never . . . never . . . never."

"One 'never' would be sufficient, dear." Another eagle

stepped closer to Dunwattle. She twisted her neck around. "Elgore, don't frighten the poor thing." She turned to Dunwattle. "Now, dearie, take a deep breath and explain your mission."

Taking a deep breath around these meat eaters seemed risky, but Dunwattle did as he was told.

"Well, yes, we do know about an egg. You see, ma'am—"

"You may call me Bess. And Elgore is my mate." *Bess and Elgore, very odd names,* Dunwattle thought.

"Yes, Bess." *Oh dear, it rhymes—yes, Bess. Don't be distracted,* Dunwattle thought. "You see, Bess, we're from Glendunny, a pond in the far hills of Scotland."

"Yes, we know Glendunny," Elgore said in his sonorous voice that rumbled like a thunderous gale. Every word this eagle uttered sounded as if it were a warning of something terrible. But Dunwattle continued.

"Our . . . our . . . swan . . ." A shiver went through the nest. The fine dusty white head feathers on all six eagles suddenly bristled, making their heads seem twice as large.

"*Your* swan?" Elgore cocked his head slightly. "By what right do you call this bird your swan?"

"Well," Locksley said quickly, "not just ours, but the pond's swan."

"Makes no difference." Elgore sniffed haughtily. "No creature, no species owns another."

"Elgore!" Bess honked loudly. "Lighten up. You're missing the point here."

"And what might be the point, my dear?"

"The point is the connection here. The feather and the egg. These young'uns are searching for a swan. It was the swan that brought the egg to the beavers of Belle d'Eau. That is the connection between the feather and the egg."

"Oh," Elgore said. The bristle of feathers on his head flattened instantly. "You're right, my dear. The egg, a swan brought that egg and then the Belle d'Eau beavers reported to us that it had gone missing." It was clear to Dunwattle and the other two kits who had the brains in this family—Bess! Her mate, Elgore, was definitely a bit dim.

"Stolen! The egg was stolen, Elgore," Bess snapped. "Gone missing makes it sound as if it flew off on its own or just walked away. The egg was a swan egg. As such it doesn't have legs or wings."

Yrynn began to speak. "But they said if anyone would know about the egg or the swan we seek, it would be you—the eagles of Iolaire." Her voice was almost pleading.

"But we know nothing," another eagle offered.

"I think it's time to call Luna." The words came from a smaller eagle, and then there was a quick whispered exchange among them. The kits didn't understand a word. It was as if they were speaking an entirely different language.

"Wh-what are you saying?" Locksley asked.

"Oh sorry, my dear," Bess said. "We're speaking in our species language. It's called Accipit. You see, there are three different 'families' in our order of birds of prey. The family that we belong to is called Accipitridae—in the old language it means large birds with strongly hooked bills." To demonstrate, she turned her head in profile. "You see, my bill is perfectly designed for killing." And all three kits grew a bit weak in their legs at this. *Carnivores could be so . . . so blunt, despite their sharp beaks or teeth,* Yrynn thought.

They could finish us off in a minute, Dunwattle realized as he imagined that beak ripping open his belly from his skeat to his throat.

"But this swan you speak of, and this feather?" Bess continued, tipping her head to one side. The light had softened in her yellow eyes.

"Yes, Elwyn our teacher said that you found some feathers too."

"Ah Elwyn. Of course." Bess nodded.

"What's 'of course' about it?" Elgore suddenly was bristling again.

"Elgore dearest, Elwyn is the beaver I told you about. He knows more about watercourses than we ever will in a lifetime. He's a beaver after all. Don't get jealous, dear. He's not my type. Not at all. But the connection is quite clear now. I have found some swan feathers in my various flyovers while attempting to keep an eye on New Eden."

"New Eden!" all three kits blurted out. "The Dark Place?"

"Indeed, it is."

"But what is it?"

A smaller eagle bustled forward. "As I said before, 'Time to call Luna!'" This eagle's eyes were a dark brown and not yellow.

"Indeed! Time to call Luna," Elgore said. He turned to the small eagle. "Albie, will you do us the honor?" He then turned to Bess. "And can you prepare the moon bowl, my dear?"

"Certainly!"

The kits watched the eagles carefully as they awaited the arrival of Luna. The birds were all tipping their heads toward the sky as they watched the last shreds of storm clouds race across the moon. They began whispering in a mixture of their old tongue and bits of the more familiar language that the kits could understand: *eeen bina elkomyn ... ni ni ... no full moon need ... no quarter ... Eyree qunca ... vlorris ... Luna postyl ... she always does ... no matter the cirrus ... kynnog ...*

The kits suddenly heard a fluttering sound, a rather loud fluttering. But as the bird landed, they were surprised to see not an eagle, but a tiny owl, the tiniest owl they had ever seen.

"This is Luna." The young eagle Albie nodded to the kits.

"She's an owl?" Locksley said.

"Of course I'm an owl!" the bird squeaked.

"But you're so small. Small I mean compared to other owls we've seen."

The tiny owl blinked and seemed to roll her eyes a bit. "Owls come in all sizes. I'm a pygmy owl. Northern pygmy, to be exact. I hunt . . ." She paused. "I hunt very well, I might add. I'm a very efficient hunter. I use hollows to stash my food. But sometimes I hang it out to dry on limbs."

"And what may I ask is your prey?" Locksley asked.

Dunwattle rolled his eyes. *Don't encourage this owl*, he wanted to say. A blabber beak if he ever saw one.

"Mostly songbirds."

"Songbirds!" all three kits shrieked.

"Oh good grief. Here we go again," Luna muttered, then sighed deeply. "Look, we all have to eat and very few of us are like you, who enjoy a diet of wood, weed, and bark."

"I ate a worm once by mistake," Locksley said.

"That hardly counts," Luna said dismissively. "But how did you like it?"

"It didn't taste that bad, but it gave me gas."

A little toot came from Luna. "You mean a fart like that?"

"Yes," Locksley replied. And Yrynn thought how Luna

must think herself so witty. Next she'd be telling poop jokes. The lowest form of humor in Yrynn's mind.

Dunwattle moaned. What a know-it-all this owl was.

"That one was brought to you by a warbler I just consumed," Luna chirped.

The kits looked at each other. *Are we supposed to thank her for that?* Dunwattle wondered with disgust.

"Anyhow, we should get on with the business at hand." Luna swiveled her head. It was almost dizzying to watch her. "So, Bess, Elgore, what's this all about?"

"Well, we need a moon reading. I realize there is not much of a moon out there tonight."

"Bess, you still don't get it, do you? If I told you once, I've told you a thousand times. I don't need the whole moon out there to read, or even a sliver. And it doesn't matter in the least if it's cloudy. You seek an egg and a feather, right?"

"That is correct," Bess answered. "We believe there is a vital connection between the two."

"Do you have the reflecting cup?"

"Yes, Luna," another eagle spoke, and pushed forward a hollowed-out burl that had been cut from a nearby tree. The burl contained water.

"All right. Now we must just line this up on the same angle as the moon, which you cannot see. But I shall soon feel that angle with my extraordinarily sensitive brain and its ability to orient itself on even the darkest and stormiest of nights."

Oh, Great Castor, Dunwattle thought. *I might just have to smack this revolting little owl.*

Luna then turned to the small eagle who had brought her the reflecting cup.

"Albie, you will follow my head movements and make all the necessary adjustments to the reflecting cup as I close my eyes. We must have complete silence as I seek the magnetic lines of the earth, as they intercept with those of the moon. Silence, please, as I start my initial exercise to prepare my mind and body." Luna spread her wings. "I shall begin with the breath of Hoole exercises honoring heaven and earth, or 'glaumora,' as we owls call heaven." The owl spread her tiny wings and began waving them rhythmically. "And now for the harmony of air and water; egg and feather." She angled her wings ever so slightly. The sky, thick with clouds, momentarily cleared, and although Luna's eyes were closed, her body began to tremble. A riffle of wind passed through her feathers, and she stared into the cup of water, where a trickle of moonlight did appear.

She began speaking in a peculiar voice, a lovely voice really, which made Dunwattle wonder if somehow the warbler she had recently consumed was singing or warbling from inside her. "They are apart . . . the egg and the feather . . . far apart . . . yes, the swan brought the egg, but the egg is in New Eden—" Her voice caught and tears began to leak from her eyes. "And . . . and . . . and the swan is far, far away from New Eden . . . on an island. . . . She is wounded but cared for by . . . by . . . yes, a two-leg! And her name is Glencora!"

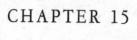

CHAPTER 15

"Forgetting Is the Coward's Way"

The young otters Edy and Iglemore had learned a lot since they had arrived in this strange and dark place. So far, they had learned that the two-legs who walked the metal walkways were called guards. Blekka explained their job was to keep the creatures in their various pools or pens and they were the ones who put the capsules in their food. "They are our jailers," Blekka had said. The words "jail" and "jailer" had to be explained to them too. Blekka the octopus was their main teacher, as it was easiest for her to get around. She was almost magical in the way she could slip from pool to pool and slither and ooze her way through the ducts, tubes, and passageways of New Eden.

Yes, they had learned that this dark place was called

New Eden. But its full name was New Eden—the Behavioral Institute for Warrior Creatures. In truth they were warrior prisoners. They would be trained to destroy things. And if they died in the process, no medals of honor were given. But nevertheless, there was hope to be found. From Blekka and from the orca Hvala, the otters learned that there was something coming that was simply called E-Day. Escape Day. On this day the creatures of New Eden would rise up. Blekka and Hvala were the chief strategists. Blekka was also the chief engineer, for she was the smartest of all the species. She had learned everything there was to know about the systems, the water pumps, the underwater passageways, and the portals that were locked and could be opened only by certain codes.

And that was the reason for Blekka's visit on this particular evening as she oozed into pool 54.

"Blekka dear, so nice to see you," Glory said. "What brings you here at this hour? Most unusual time for you."

"I wish I could say unusual circumstances, but unfortunately not."

"You are flushed, a most beautiful shade of pink."

"It is in honor of Inia—in memoriam, I should say."

"Pink! Pink is . . . is gone."

Blekka bowed her head. "Yes. Pink is gone."

"B-b-but . . . b-but . . . ," both pups stammered. They had

become very close to the dolphin. She would come almost every night to give them bubble shows. If Blekka was the storyteller, Pink was their magician. She could blow bubble pictures in the shape of any cloud they asked for.

"But what happened?" Glory asked.

"I had hoped that I would not have occasion to tell you this so soon. But here we are." She flopped four or five of her arms as if to say, *What's one to do?* "You see, all of us here are being trained. Soon you will also be trained to be part of a secret program to detect bombs and other military weapons that might be underwater, in order to protect New Eden military sites. You might even be trained to deliver bombs. They often attach cameras to some animals for spy missions." *Bombs? Weapons? Spy missions?* All of these words were unfamiliar to Glory and her pups. They had to be explained by Blekka, who was very patient.

"So," Glory said. "Does this have to do with Pink being a missile?"

"Indeed," Blekka murmured, and her voice broke.

"How did she die?" Glory asked.

"The bomb she was carrying had been programmed to slip off beneath a British ship, but it exploded early. And . . . and . . ." The water in the pool was now tumultuous with Blekka's waving arms undulating every which way. "But I am here only to warn you that at feeding time, which will be soon, there is a new capsule you must look out for. It's green."

"And what does this one do?" Glory narrowed her eyes.

"It is the forgetting capsule. It will make you forget Pink."

"Never!" all three otters said at once. No more magic. No more bubble clouds. But they would never forget Pink.

"I shan't forget her either," said a voice they had not heard before.

"Who said that?" Glory was suddenly alert. The voice was familiar. She'd heard that voice before. Where? She swam quickly to the far side of the pool and looked through one of the viewing windows.

"Levi!" she gasped. "Levi, son of Rolf and Twigga?"

"Yes, yes, and I am so ashamed. That is why I have hidden in my pool ever since you arrived. I dared not swim near this window."

"What is it, dear?" Glory asked. "The guards are on break now. Tell us what happened to make you ashamed. However did you come to this awful place?"

And so, Levi, clasping his front legs over the rim of the wading pool, told the dreadful tale of how he had joined the dishonorable beavers of Glendunny to try to hunt down Dunwattle for his crime of vysculf.

"Yes, I survived, but I can never go back. I am so ashamed. Never never ever go back. I can die here. I wish I would die instead of Pink."

"Now don't you dare say that. You can go back. Never say 'never'!"

Levi looked at the feisty little otter in wonder. How could she not hate him? How could anybody ever like him, or even love him, again? "But no one could trust me."

"I trust you," Glory said. She squinted her eyes at him. "Did you swallow your food tonight? Did you swallow that forgetting capsule?" She didn't wait for him to answer but leapt over the partition to the pool he occupied and rammed him hard in the stomach. He uppled and the little green capsule floated to the surface.

"No forgetting for you, young'un. You must remember Pink. Forgetting is the easy way out. The coward's way out. We must all remember Pink to honor her and to keep our wits about us. For we are getting out of here. When E-Day comes, we shall be ready. This place that they call New Eden is the foulest and most soul-destroying place on earth. These two-legs are the evilest of all two-legs in their tyranny against all creatures no matter what their species. But it's going to end!"

"But I don't deserve to live." Levi's voice quavered. "I need to forget and then—"

"Nonsense. To live is not to forget. To forget is to die with shame. You must keep calm and carry on! That is your only choice." Glory had narrowed her eyes and a fierce light radiated from them. The kits had never seen their mother so angry. But they knew she was not mad at them or at Levi. She was mad at the world.

CHAPTER 16

Two Brains, One Spirit

On that early morning on Little Feidah, Glencora had been stirred in her sleep. It was as if something called to her in her sleep—*vertu-zel*. Whatever did those words mean? But she felt as though she had been blessed. As if that swan had whispered something directly into her ear. But that could not be. She was in bed in her bedroom and the swan was in the cupola of the barn.

She roused herself from sleep and at the window caught the last glimpse of the swan, her wings spread and slightly angled as she carved a turn and headed north. "Free!" Glencora whispered, and joy flooded through the old lady as she watched the swan begin to dissolve into a bank of filmy cirrus clouds. She was flying steadily on an east wind, two points or so off her right wing. That wing had healed and soon she would be able to catch the westerlies that would give her a boost of speed.

But Glencora wondered if she herself had actually somehow entered the deep schwanka, as some called the swan's special sleep. And if this had occurred, what exactly had she glimpsed that was stirring in this swan—this nameless swan's mind? For despite the intimacy that had brought them so close, Glencora had no idea of her name. Both she and Lachlan had simply called her "swan." And yet in some mysterious way, a wordless way, they had shared so much. There was no denying that somehow the old woman and the swan had merged and become one, if not physically at least spiritually. Hence a peculiar transmission of thought had begun to occur. But this much Glencora knew—the swan had to return to her origins, in a place called Wyntersphree. Yes, the name had come to her as if in a dream. Wyntersphree. There, far up a fjord, was a nearby pond, and on its banks was an empty nest.

If the swan could reach this place, she would find fragments of a broken code. And when she pieced them together, she could go on to find something she might have lost. Now that was all Glencora sensed. But she herself had been a code breaker in the last great war. To break a code, one had to study the cipher, the disguised way of writing a code. There were systems for doing this, like counting how many times a letter occurred or the use of certain words. In this way a pattern could be detected, a scheme of some sort. It was a step-by-step procedure that broke down the seeming randomness of letters or symbols so that a design began to emerge and become readable. This was how code breakers worked.

Now of course for the swan, the pattern would not be letters or symbols but fragments of information—a piece of moss that had cushioned the egg when it was in the nest, a twig, sedges, plant material from the pond. These were the building blocks of the nest, and perhaps if the swan was lucky, there might be the wisp of a feather. Although swans were not known for their ability to detect smells the way land animals were, these things would make an image in their heads that was as good as a map.

In some strange way, Glencora was certain that the swan appeared to be searching for something, and for this she had to go back to the beginning—the very beginning—of a very convoluted journey. How often had Glencora Barrington herself had to go back to the beginnings when she was a young woman working as a spy and a code breaker? Countless times. All she had to do then was stay calm and carry on, and eventually she would crack the code. And so would the swan.

The way the wind riffled through Elsinore's plummels, the fluffy micro-feathers that grew between the swan's flight feathers, felt different—drier, and they bore a new scent with a tinge of salt. *And they say we can't smell!* Elsinore thought. *This old sniffer of mine knows fjord salt.* The difference in the salt was that it mingled with the scent of the granite walls of the long Sansa fjord that she was flying up now. As she approached the end of the fjord, she began carving a turn to port. There was the pond ahead. The tundra moss was in full bloom surrounding the pond. The sedges thickened toward the east side of the pond and would be delectable this time of year. However, she should be looking not forward, but back. She had come to reawaken her senses—her "hind" sense as it was when she had first found the egg in the empty nest. There was much about a swan's brain of which scientists knew nothing. There was a kind of secret compartment, somewhere between the nerves, that related to eye motions and those for adjusting flight feathers. This brain stored lasting impressions. As swans grew older, they became more mature. And with more experiences they became increasingly adept at engaging this secret compartment and searching it for long-buried memories and sensations. Elsinore now came in for a landing as one part of that secret compartment began to open. A thought came to her in a vibrant red color, soft and luxuriant. But was this hindsight or now? Seconds before she landed, she realized it was *now*! This was not a memory at all. It was happening. It was present, not past. She was peering into the bright yellow eyes of a red fox! Its bushy red tail tipped in black was lifted and curled. Its ears were flattened. It leapt into the air, high enough to reach Elsinore's wing tip! This was not hindsight, this was NOW. *No! NO! NOT MY WING!* This was happening. And in her brain, there was a collision of sounds—the barks and screeches of foxes. The swirl of feathers and, yes, blood.

On Little Feidah Island, as Glencora Barrington was pouring tea for Lachlan, something caused her to spill a bit. "Sorry about that." She set down the cup of tea.

"Something wrong, dear?" Lachlan asked, looking over the top of the newspaper he was reading. He noticed a slight tremor in her hand.

"I . . . I . . . I think our swan is in trouble."

PART THREE

The
Drop

CHAPTER 17

The Most Silent of Fliers

In this same moment back at Big Nest, Luna the pygmy owl seemed to have entered a deep trance. Her tiny wings quivered, and her eyes had a mad light as another high, melodic voice issued from her. *That of a songbird?* the kits wondered and shuddered at the thought of the songbird she had recently consumed singing from within her tiny body.

"And . . . and . . . and the swan is far, far away from New Eden . . . on an island. . . . She is wounded but cared for by . . . by . . . yes, a two-leg! And her name is Glencora!" There was a long pause. The kits looked at Luna attentively, almost desperate for her next utterance. "Yes, but, but . . . now . . . the swan is beyond the help of Glencora. . . ."

The words rang shrill in the three kits' ears.

"Who in the world is Glencora?" Yrynn asked in a hoarse whisper.

"Glen-what-a?" Dunwattle asked, mystified by the name.

Locksley sniffed. "Sounds very two-legs to me."

"Two-leg, three-leg, four-leg, what's the use?" Dunwattle moaned.

"Don't whine, Dunwattle," Yrynn said.

"I wasn't whining. I was moaning," Dunwattle snapped. "So, what should we do, Yrynn? Seems to me the only choice is to go back to Glendunny and say we have failed."

Luna seemed to wake from her trance. "You can't fail if you haven't even tried," she said. "All I did was tell you that the swan is far away from New Eden and wounded and on an island. And the name Glencora just came into my head. The swan might be healed by now. She might be flying toward you . . . or away, perhaps to even greater danger. Mind you, I'm not certain. My art, the science of reading moon reflections, is not an exact one. My information just comes to me in garbled bits and pieces. Being a moon reader isn't precisely science, nor is it purely art, you know."

"Yes, I think we can assume that," Locksley said, barely concealing his contempt.

Yrynn was embarrassed by her friends. Locksley was sounding so snooty, and Dunwattle had dissolved into a whining wreck. *So emotional!* Yrynn thought.

Luna had been standing by, listening to their bickering.

She had recovered her normal tone. There was no trace of the songbird. "It seems to me," she began in her little piping voice, "that you three are not putting two and two together."

"How's that?" Locksley huffed grumpily.

The little owl turned and picked a nit out of her flight feathers. "When you are as small as I am, you can't carry any extra weight." She looked now at all three, which she did efficiently by spinning her head around in a dizzying whirl. It made the kits slightly nauseated. "I know, it always disturbs creatures when we do this. It's the extra bones in our neck and spine that allow us to do it." She spun her head one more time to demonstrate. "We are the only birds who have this particular talent. Impressive, isn't it?"

"If you insist," murmured Yrynn. She was thinking she could impress this little pygmy owl with her broad, flat tail and swat Luna to kingdom come. But of course, she wouldn't. The little bird was only trying to help them. "Can we get back to putting two and two together?"

"Yes, of course. I have a tendency to digress." She cleared her throat now. "You say you have failed, but how can you fail if you haven't even tried yet?"

"But we have tried," Yrynn protested.

"No, you haven't," Luna said crisply.

"Huh?" Dunwattle grunted.

"You have one egg." Luna lifted her port wing. "And

you have one swan. Now what is the connection?"

"But the egg doesn't have anything to do with us," Dunwattle argued.

"With you?!" There was a slightly scathing note in Luna's voice. "But it could have something to do with Elsinore. She's a swan. The egg is a swan egg after all."

Locksley's whiskers began to quiver. "You're not suggesting that Elsinore . . . our Elsinore—" His voice broke. "That the egg is her egg? That she has a mate, and they had an egg together?" Shock radiated from his dark eyes.

"Don't look so astonished. It's possible, but I myself don't think the egg was hers. Why would she bring it here to the pond of Belle d'Eau and not your pond?"

"Yes, our pond!" Dunwattle gasped. "We would have helped her with rearing the little guy."

"Guy?" Yrynn said. "Dunwattle, why are you using a two-leg word, a human word, like 'little guy' to describe a chick of a swan? They are called cygnets, by the way."

Luna regarded Yrynn carefully. She was a smart one. She realized her only hope lay with this kit. So, she spun her head once more. And then zeroed in on Yrynn.

"You all need to think about this place, New Eden, where we feel the swan egg was taken. Think about these beavers who were charged with caring for this egg. The egg given to them by your friend Elsinore."

"Well, we're not sure about that," Locksley protested.

"Whether it was her egg or not doesn't matter at this point. The idea is to bring the swan and the egg back together again."

This idea was almost unthinkable for the kits. Each kit felt that Elsinore was theirs and not to be shared.

"But how do we do that?" Dunwattle asked.

"I feel that you need to drop in."

"Drop in where?"

"New Eden."

Silence descended on the kits. The idea was simply preposterous. Locksley jutted his head forward.

"Just drop into this evil place? And how do you propose doing it?" Locksley asked. The little owl barely came up to his nose.

"Exactly as I said. Drop in. 'Drop' is the operative word here, my friends."

Yrynn now spoke. "May I remind you, Luna, that we have already been dropped into the eagles' nest by the eagles? And quite frankly we didn't much care for the ride! Except for the scenery. It was a bit rough and Dunwattle nearly uppled! Why would we want to do this again? And especially into a place you say is evil." And what she didn't say was, *Why would we save an egg for Elsinore, when she had already decided to not foster it herself, but just give it away?*

"Why? To save the world. That's why."

The three kits might be for saving the world, but why

did this egg have to be involved?

"But they'll see us coming," Dunwattle said. "They'll hear us coming. We'll be dead before we get there. I know the eagles are strong, but honestly they are noisy fliers."

"But you see, it won't be eagles who will drop you in."

"Then who will it be?" Yrynn asked.

"Owls," Luna replied simply.

"Owls!" all three kits exclaimed.

"You?" Locksley said. "You, Luna? You don't weigh as much as my front paw."

"Not me, silly. You think owls only come in one size, in one species?"

"Well, we haven't seen that many, at least not in Glen-dunny where we are from."

"That's just the point. You don't see them because you can't. Owls are masters of camouflage. And most impor-tantly they are the most silent fliers on earth." Luna paused a bit. "Or I should say above the earth, in the air." The little pygmy grew very still and then began a slow swivel of her head. She appeared to be scanning the slim trees in the grove of the forest where they had met in the eagles' tree. "I can count at least fifteen right here in this grove. Over there in that cluster of birch trees." Luna pointed with the tip of her wing.

"What?"

"They are there. Fifteen snowies. They are what we call

'wilfing.' It's part of a fear response, the courage part of fear."

The courage part of fear. The word rang ominously in Dunwattle's ears. He had never thought of fear as having parts. Was he courageous when he went crashing over those falls? No, he was just stupid! What could be the courage part of fear?

Luna continued. "You see, kits, at this moment those owls are not fearful at all. They are simply blending in with the tree—more specifically the bark of those birch trees, which is a mottled gray and white. Those snowies have not fully fledged. If they had, they would be completely white. So, at this stage they're a perfect match for the bark of a birch tree. Camouflage! And over there in the hickory tree with its rough bark—is it gray? Is that bark black, with a touch of tawny? Look who blends in perfectly!"

"Who?" all three kits said at once.

"A great gray owl, fully fledged but a perfect match, and still the great gray has stretched herself slender, slender as the limb on which she perches. Indistinguishable from the other branches."

The three kits tipped their heads back and looked up at the tree. "I don't see anything," Yrynn said.

"Well, that is the point of camouflage. But see that branch halfway down?" Luna asked.

"Yeah. Nothing on that branch," Dunwattle said.

"Look just below the branch." The three kits squinted harder.

"Oh . . . ," Locksley said softly, and then the others saw the shape. It was an owl!

"It really is so skinny," Dunwattle gasped.

"And so tall," Yrynn added.

"Great grays are one of the larger species of owls. But this fellow Nebby has stretched himself quite long—increased his normal height by at least a third. It's called wilfing."

"Wilfing?" Yrynn asked.

"And as I told you, it's actually a fear reaction. But he's not fearful now. Nebby has used fear as a camouflage. With his length and the natural color of his feathers he has disguised himself. The formal name of his species is *Strix nebulosa*."

"Nebulosa?" Locksley asked.

"A fancy word for cloudy. Perfect for undercover ops! That is why the great grays will be the ones to drop you into New Eden."

"Not the eagles like before?" Dunwattle asked.

"Never," Luna said emphatically. "Not only do eagles lack camouflage, but they are noisy fliers. On a cloudy night you'll never be able to see a bird like Nebby. Nor will you hear them. Owls are the most silent fliers in the world. It's all because of their fringe feathers. Not like me. Pygmy owls might be small, but we make a big noise when flying.

What a racket! But with fringe feathers, it's as if the air is greased and they simply slide through it."

"But why are you so noisy?"

"No fringe feathers. Therefore, no undercover work for us. But barred owls are also great for camouflage operations. So, a team of both great grays and barred might drop you in."

Locksley looked at his two friends. The question was clear in his eyes. *So, they just assume we've agreed to all this?*

And we're not exactly thin, thought Dunwattle. *We're chubby. Un-wilfable*, he thought as he glimpsed his own rotund shadow in the last sliver of moonlight.

CHAPTER 18

Written on the Wind

Far up the Wyntersphree fjord over the island of Eyja Svane, the air churned with sudden gale-force drafts of wind. But it was no gale. It was the power of Elsinore's wings. *I'm back! I've healed!* She shot straight up into the sky, beyond the reach of the fox. She watched as another fox staggered out of the brush. What was wrong with this fox? It was as if his legs weren't working right. She now noticed that it was the same with the other fox. Yet both continued leaping as if trying to snatch her from the air, but she was far beyond their reach. She rose even higher on a warm draft of air and continued to hover out of their reach, as there was something mesmerizing about their convulsive and futile leaping as they tried to claw the air beneath her.

Then Elsinore glimpsed something else. Threads of foam like scribbles on the wind spun through the air. She felt her gizzard clench. *Great Svanka!* The foaming mouth disease! It was written on the wind. This must have been why the egg was abandoned by its parents. They had either died themselves of the disease or fled the nest in fear. But none of these dreadful signals, these intimations of death, were here when she had first found the egg nearly a month before. Or had she just missed them? She would have noticed. But perhaps not. Perhaps both parents had been attacked far from the nest. They usually took turns guarding the nest. She began to imagine one swan disappearing and then the other swan going in search and finding these foxes or another deadly foaming mouth creature. When the foaming mouth disease came to the fjord, it often spread rapidly into a plague.

By the time Elsinore came along on her first visit when she found the egg, there would not have been a trace of the disease close to the nest. So, she found the egg untouched but destined to die if it hatched in this abandoned state. And so, she had taken it to the beavers of Belle d'Eau. It would not be the first time a different species fostered an egg until it hatched. But could the parents of this egg have been swept up in the disease back then? Was the egg not abandoned willfully but instead the parents snatched by death?

She recalled so clearly the night she had been brought to the pond of Belle d'Eau—a stormy night with just a sliver of a waning moon. The beavers were in their lodges, sound asleep, for work had been hampered by the weather. Nevertheless, that empty muskrat's nest caught in a splinter of moonlight seemed almost to be beckoning for the egg. Elsinore decided to leave it for the pond, safely tucked into the nest with some additional moss. The beavers of Belle d'Eau would know what to do. She had watched them from afar for months now. They were clever. They were kind, and they were wise to keep their existence a secret from the beavers of Glendunny.

But now Elsinore was certain that the egg was lost yet again. The vacancy in that muskrat nest seemed to reverberate through her. She didn't need to see it to feel it. And this time she knew that the egg had been not abandoned but stolen! Yes, stolen! Of this she was certain. Now why would any creature want to steal a swan egg from a nest? Especially a nest protected by beavers.

Elsinore flew off and began a wide circling of the land beyond the nest. And she found more evidence of the dreadful foaming mouth disease. This certainly explained why the parents had abandoned the nest, leaving behind the egg. They most likely thought they could return at some point but then had become sick themselves. There were many more bodies of animals that had died or were dying across the rugged landscape. Soon she came near another pond where she found the bones of two swans. Would she know for sure that these were the parents of the egg? Perhaps never. But one thing Elsinore did know was that she had done the right thing in taking that egg far, far away. The moment of that decision came back to her. It was so vivid. She had decided to carry the egg across the vast sea of Wyntersphree, to the high mountain pond of Belle d'Eau.

Belle d'Eau had been her secret . . . well, a secret between her and Elwyn, the elderly beaver of Glendunny who was one of the kits' favorite teachers.

Elwyn, the teacher of hydrology, who knew more about water and watercourses than any fish. She had discovered the Canadian beavers some years before and had told no one except for Elwyn. She had been reluctant to tell anyone at Glendunny, but she and Elywn were quite close. Elsinore had often wondered if they had been born the same species if they might have become mates. It always seemed so odd to her that they had been drawn to one another. She a creature of air and he of water. He a teacher of water hydraulics and she a master of air hydraulics, as he called it. He had always scoffed at her for saying that they came from such different realms. "Air, water, my dear, not as much of a difference as you might think. The principles are the same. It's all about pressure, the properties of air and water." But he promised to keep her secret quiet, her discovery of the Castors of Belle d'Eau.

But Elsinore had never told him about the egg. He had never even inquired if Belle d'Eau had a swan. She felt he might have assumed it did. The idea of a swan-less pond was unimaginable for beavers, even one as intelligent as Elwyn.

Now that she thought about it, she missed them all, Elwyn and especially Dunwattle, Locksley, and the little orphan Yrynn. Were the kits still alive? That horrible scene in the cedar forest came back to her. The lynx leaping into that tree where she had perched. The searing pain of her wing being ripped, the drenching blood—how had she ever escaped? With such grievous wounds, how had she ever flown so far as to arrive in Skibodeen, the estate of the woman called Glencora? But she knew now that Glencora was a friend, a soul mate. *Felajvel* was the word in Old Swan. The compass in her brain realigned itself now with the compass in her heart and her soul, and she flew on, a direct course to Belle d'Eau. For it was all written on the wind. And she would find that stolen egg.

CHAPTER 19

Beavers in Trees
and Other Oddities

It's all so different, Dunwattle thought. So different from the flight when they were seized by the eagles. He was hanging from the talons of the great gray owl named Nebby. The air they were passing through was silken. The speed was much slower than their flight with the eagles. There was no rackety sound or the harsh sibilant whistling noise as there had been with the eagles as they angled their wings into the wind. There was only utter silence, and that in itself was mesmerizing for the kits.

The three were suspended from the talons of three slightly different owls.

"Some call these clouds nebulous. Like our species *Strix nebulosa* and my name—Nebby. Get it?" said the large gray-and-white owl carrying Dunwattle.

"Yes," Dunwattle replied softly, but in truth he didn't quite get it.

"And some call it a sheep-back sky, you know, with woolly clouds. We're certainly not sheep. Ha! Feathers, not wool. It's a joke," said the great gray called Flint, who was transporting Yrynn. "But we do match the sky," he added.

"Not much of a joke, Flint," replied another owl, Maggs, who was carrying Locksley.

"But what kind of an owl are you?" Yrynn asked. For she was clearly not a great gray. "You in between?" For Maggs's colors were not really gray at all, but brown, with just a touch of light misty white and perhaps a hint of red.

"I suppose you could say that I'm in between, but it would not truly describe my spectrum, which is profound and subtle."

Locksley didn't know how colors could be profound. "So in between what?" Locksley asked, looking up at Maggs's tawny belly feathers.

"I'm a great horned owl and my feathers have a range of colors. I can be in the spectrum of the dawn, the minute before the sun rises, and then the last glow of the sunset. As the dusk sets in and the sun is swallowed. Depending on how I ruffle my feathers I can match those sky events of sunrise and sunset exactly. I can get the tint just right. I am somewhat of an artist."

"Don't we know it," Nebby churred. This was an owl's way of laughing. "Maggs here will remind you of this several times a day."

"Give me a dusk in the northern light, I'll match it. Give me two seconds after the break of day, I'm your owl! And oh, give me a night of Red Sprites and I'm magic!"

"What are Red Sprites?" Yrynn asked.

"They're coming," Maggs said.

"That is why she is invaluable to us in the coming nights." Flint twisted his head toward Maggs as he spoke. "For it will soon be the time of the Red Sprites."

"Red Sprites?" Dunwattle asked. "Are they birds too?"

All three owls churred now.

"Red Sprites happen high above the nimbus—the cumulonimbus clouds. And when we find them this time of year, they are always above thunderstorms. The thunderstorms are a nursery, so to speak, for these Red Sprites—a special kind of lightning."

"What does it look like when the Red Sprites come?" Locksley asked.

"Well," Nebby said, "the night must be moonless for them to show up the best."

Flint paused, trying to find a word. "They are like

lightning, but not exactly. They are more luminous, and more beautiful. Not simply white like lightning, but almost a rose color, a deep red."

Maggs broke in. "See my port coverts, on my primary feathers? They are a perfect match for Red Sprites."

Suddenly the air was seized by a tremendous noise. It was as if the whole sky trembled.

"What? What?" Dunwattle screeched.

"Alter course two degrees to port, descend quarter league," Flint called out.

"Nothing to worry about, just a plane," Maggs said. "We can avoid them."

"A plane?" Locksley asked. "What's a plane?"

"Flying machine," Nebby said. An immense silver shape whizzed overhead, leaving a bit of a tumult in the air.

"Hang on," Maggs said.

Us hang on? Yrynn thought as she looked up at the talons gripping her. *That's their job, not ours.*

"And don't miss the show of the Red Sprites. Red Sprites truly bring out the painter in me," Maggs said.

"But what else besides their color do these sprites look like exactly?" Dunwattle asked.

"There's no *exactly* with Red Sprites," Nebby said. "They come in all shapes. They can look like fire—a forest fire raging across the sky. Or a waterfall of bright red cinders. But often they look like a flower blooming, spreading its petals against the night."

"Or an octopus," Maggs broke in.

"An octo-what?" Locksley asked.

"You don't know what an octopus is?" Flint said.

"No," all three said at once.

"Well, you will know soon enough." Nebby's voice was slow and slightly ominous.

"Is it scary?" Yrynn whispered.

"It depends." Nebby seemed to be thinking as he spoke. "But this octopus is probably the smartest creature you'll ever meet."

"You'll meet her soon," Maggs added.

"It's a her?" Yrynn asked.

"Hard to tell with an octopus," Flint said, "but yes, Blekka is a female."

They flew on for another five leagues in the splendid darkness of this silken night hung with stars.

"Coming in for a landing in the rowan tree. Two points off to styrbor," Maggs called out.

The kits felt the owls carving a wide turn as they headed toward a large tree.

Styrbor, that must be the opposite of port, all three kits thought. They were quickly learning the language of air creatures. Port was one side, styrbor was the other.

Ahead they saw an immense tree, unlike any they had ever seen before.

"Beautiful, isn't it?" Flint sighed. Then Nebby gave a series of hoots.

"Unit three coming in. Heavy cargo." The hoot was deep, low, and very resonant.

"Read you, unit three," an anonymous voice called back.

"Requesting instructions for landing."

"Third branch beneath the understory. North side of tree."

The owls with their heavy cargo circled the tree once before beginning their long, silent glide toward the landing branch. Yrynn watched. She focused her attention on the leading edges of the flight feathers combed with the fluffy tufts called plummels. "Velvet" was the word that popped into Yrynn's head. She had learned this word in Two-legs Vigilance class when they had studied the clothing of humans. Velvet was a very soft, luxuriant fabric that rich ladies like the queen of England wore. And now Yrynn felt rich. She felt folded into the silent wind with these velvet plummels of the owl brushing her face. *I feel like a queen!* she thought to herself. *Majestic!*

And it was a beautiful moment when they landed. The tree was immense. They had never before seen such a large tree. Not even in the cedar woods where the ancient trees grew to enormous sizes over thousands of years. A light snow cloaked the branches, but on those branches was something even whiter than snow. But the kits were unsure

what this whiteness was exactly. Although it was a moonless night, the tree itself appeared luminous. It took the kits
a moment or two or maybe even three to comprehend what
they were actually seeing.

It was in fact something they had heard about—a parliament of owls, of snowy owls to be specific. Just as there
were colonies of beavers and schools of fish or a flutter
of butterflies and what Elsinore had called a *lamentation* of
swans. This was what a cluster of owls was called, a parliament. It sounded so important. Beavers by comparison were
so boring, Dunwattle thought. His inner poet was offended.
A colony, what did that mean? Parliament was something
important. In Two-legs Vigilance class they'd learned that
in England the real boss was not the queen, but a group of
two-legs called the Parliament. They made the laws for a
whole country!

The kits looked about them in awe as they were gently
set down on three different branches.

"And what have we here?" asked one large female, a
snowy.

"They are here to gnaw," Nebby replied. *Gnaw?* the kits
wondered. Gnaw down this tree? Or just trim it? They were
confused.

"Ah," replied the snowy. "Blekka will be pleased!"

"Indeed," echoed several of the other owls. The kits' eyes
darted about. There was something almost magical about

this moment. These stunningly beautiful owls with their snowy-white plumage appeared like enormous starry clusters that had come down from heaven and settled in the branches of the rowan tree.

"I was just going to tell them about Blekka. Or explain, as she is such a unique and complicated creature," Nebby said.

"Complicated is putting it mildly," the owl said softly, then paused. "My name is Scanda, by the way."

"Scanda," the three kits murmured. They knew that this owl must be female, because in the owl world the females were usually larger than the males. This female with her all-white plumage appeared enormous.

"And yours?" Scanda asked.

"I'm Dunwattle."

"I'm Yrynn."

"And I'm Locksley."

"Hmmm . . ." Scanda tipped her head as if considering them. "Well, let Nebby continue with his explanation of Blekka."

Nebby floated down to a branch closer to the ones the beavers were on. "Yes, octopuses are most unusual. They are boneless creatures. But what they lack in bones, they make up for in other ways. They have eight legs, or arms—tentacles, we call them. They grab like talons, but they also help them swim through the ocean."

"Eight!" the kits whispered, and looked at one another in disbelief.

"Yes, eight arms, but just one head."

Dunwattle wondered if this was supposed to make them feel better about this freakish creature.

Nebby explained the octopus's scattered brain, which could receive information from all parts of its body. "A delightfully complex creature that is incredibly intelligent. They are masters of escape and master thieves. Having eight arms certainly helps with that."

"And don't forget the hearts," an owl from above called down to Nebby.

"Oh yes, must not forget the hearts. An octopus has not one, not two, but three hearts. They are all somewhere toward the top of the octopus—if one can ever determine where the top is."

The kits were dizzy with Nebby's explanation. It was the most unimaginable creature. Even the queen of England was more imaginable to Dunwattle. With her crown, her scepter, her gowns, and her realms, she actually seemed impoverished when compared to an octopus. By comparison she was rather humdrum, especially with that little pocketbook she always carried.

The three beavers were each trying to sort things out. Finally, Locksley said, "I can't remember why we even started talking about this octopus, Blekka."

"Oh, it was the Red Sprites," Maggs piped up.

"What do Red Sprites and octopuses have in common?"

"Well," Maggs continued, "octopuses can change color—in a flash. They can go from gray to red, as red as one of my tail feathers." Maggs spun around on the limb and tipped her tail feathers at the kits.

That could be considered rude. Tipping one's butt like that, Yrynn thought. *Well, it's an upside-down world here. Whoever heard of beavers in trees?*

Maggs continued with her explanation. "The Red Sprites are lightning that appear as long, glistening threads like rain." She gave her head a spin. "So, if there are sprites tonight, it is a perfect time to smuggle Blekka out. She will match the sprites."

"Out of where?" Locksley asked.

"New Eden!" Maggs replied. "And that is where your gnawing comes in."

"Huh?" the kits said at once. For they were completely bewildered.

"Don't worry. Blekka will explain everything."

"Oh Glaux," another voice exclaimed. It seemed to belong to an immature snowy, his feathers still mottled with gray spots. "I hope so, tonight could be the night! I've never seen them."

"Now calm down, dear. You just hatched out less than a moon ago," another owl said.

Dunwattle saw the little bit of fluff that had just spoken. He was under the wing of Scanda, whom Dunwattle assumed to be his mother.

"And their ink! Poisonous," the snowy owlet added.

Blekka was sounding more monstrous by the second.

But then there was a clap of thunder. And above the dark, racing clouds, a sudden splash of red that kindled the night. The three kits tipped their heads up. Unlike birds, they were shortsighted, but they could see colors. The splash of red soon became a fire in the sky.

"They're coming! They're coming—the Red Sprites are coming!"

"And so is Blekka!" the little snowy hooted. "I see her—one, two, three, four . . ." The little owlet turned to Yrynn. "I just learned to count. I can go way beyond eight. I can count to a thousand. I'm going to count the stars."

"That might take forever," Yrynn said.

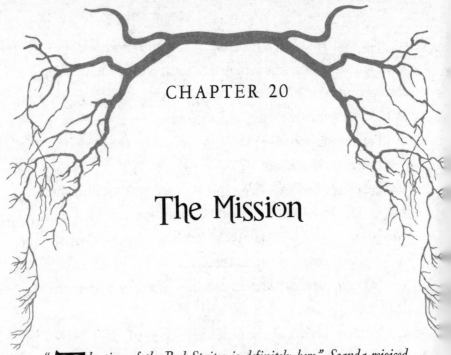

CHAPTER 20

The Mission

"The time of the Red Sprites is definitely here." Scanda rejoiced and clapped her white wings that now had a tinge of pink. "And Benjy, please calm down. You're going to toss yourself right out of this tree and you really haven't fledged all of your flight feathers yet, nor learned branching."

"Grrrrrr . . ." Benjy made a low growling noise. "Don't keep reminding me, Mum. Puleeze."

"This . . . this . . . this is magical . . . ," Yrynn said, almost swooning. She felt enveloped in the beauty of this night. She wished that in this moment she could become an owl. She tried to imagine flying on her own, not being flown by owls, but with her own wings through this night.

"This seems so beautiful to me," Yrynn whispered.

"It's not," Benjy said matter-of-factly. "The Red Sprites are actually caused by large-scale electrical discharges. They are triggered by discharges of positive lightning between an underlying thundercloud and the ground. . . ."

Someone was murmuring behind Yrynn, "Oh Glaux, if this owlet could fly as good as he can talk!"

"I heard that, Gort." Benjy's hoot now was shrill. "I'll fly when I'm ready!"

"Put your wings where your mouth is," Gort replied.

"Stop it this minute!" Scanda said, spinning her head about. "One more remark like that and it's back to your hollow, Gort."

The owl Gort dipped his head and looked instantly contrite. "Sorry."

Scanda just gave a windy harrumph.

Another owl, Gwinna, sidled up to Yrynn. She seemed quite elderly. "Benjy is just a late bloomer, like his grandfather. But he is powerfully smart. He'll grow up to be a weather reader—just like his grandfather. He just has an instinct for these things."

"Bama, I'm not a flower. I don't *bloom*. No more flower talk!"

"Well, your grandfather was a late bloomer too."

"And Bumpa is definitely late, as in dead—totally 'wilted'!"

"Well now, dearie, everyone dies."

"But Bumpa died bravely in the line of battle when the New Eden dark ops team shot him. He died with a bullet in his gizzard. He died a hero when he attacked a guard there."

"No more talk of that," Scanda said. "We must carry on."

"Yes," Nebby said. "Let's get down to business. Blekka will be arriving soon." He spun his head to the three kits.

"It kind of makes me nauseous when they spin their heads like that," Dunwattle whispered to Yrynn.

"Shush!"

"What have we gotten ourselves in for?" Locksley whispered.

Benjy now waddled up the limb where he was perched, then fluttered his wings just a tiny bit and floated down to the branch where Yrynn was wedged.

"Pardon me," he said in a tiny voice. He seemed on the brink of tears. "Sometimes I get so mad. I hate being teased. Gort is always teasing me."

"I know what you mean." Yrynn sighed, thinking back to her days at Glendunny when she was teased mercilessly because she was a Canuck.

Then there was an odd whistling sound. "What's that?" Yrynn muttered.

"Delya." The voice came from the hollow.

"Huh?" Yrynn stuck her head into the hollow. It looked rather cozy.

"Delya, she's our whistler."

"What does a whistler do?"

"A lot," Benjy said. "But she's calling everyone to attention right now, for the descent of Blekka. Then she'll explain the mission."

"What mission?"

There was a tiny giggle that emanated from the hollow.

"Your mission, silly. The gnawing mission."

Dunwattle gasped.

"What's this about a mission?" said Locksley just beneath them.

"Just listen. All will be explained." Benjy sighed. "I don't mean to be rude, but please don't bother me. I need to sulk for a while."

There were three more short whistle blasts, followed by a melodic four-note hoot: *whoop wu-hu hooooo.* Locksley felt the branch shake lightly as something landed. Something, but he was not sure what.

"Might I share this branch with you, young'un?" Locksley had to blink, for the owl seemed to blend in perfectly against the bark of the tree and the shadows of the night.

"Remarkable, isn't it? The camouflage, I mean."

"Quite," Yrynn replied.

"Yes, a gift of my species. *Strix occidentalis*, a spotted owl. That's a fancy name, but my given name is Delya. My talent is different from the great grays and the great horned or even the barred and the snowy owls. All talented in the arts of aerial camouflage—matching twilights, dusks, and dawns, and any number of cloud formations. My talent is with my abundance of spots. I can make an enemy dizzy."

Delya then gave a throat-clearing hoot as Scanda settled next to her on the branch. "Now to get on with the task at hand. I'm sure you kits are wondering what this mission is exactly."

At that moment each kit had a similar thought. They had set out to find Elsinore. Elwyn and the Aquarius both had directed them. But now it seemed as if that mission had been linked to another one. Did Elwyn and the Aquarius realize this? Eagles had been mentioned, but never owls, and certainly not an octopus!

All three kits recalled fragments of those first conversations with Elwyn and the Aquarius with startling clarity. Some white feathers, swan feathers, had been found by eagles. Thus, they had been sent to find the eagles . . . the eagles of Iolaire. But what they remembered most vividly were the dreadful words about the evil two-legs and the place far to the north. *These evil people have a fascination with creatures, creatures of all species that they can train, mold, and brainwash to do their evil work.* But Elwyn had not mentioned anything about swan eggs. And not one owl in this tree had mentioned anything about any egg either.

Before Delya could even begin, Dunwattle raised a paw. "You wish to ask a question, young'un?" the owl asked.

"Not exactly a question. But this is about the evil two-legs and that place . . ." Dunwattle paused. "New Eden."

Delya and Scanda exchanged a glance. "Indeed it is, Dunwattle," Scanda replied. "They have Levi from Glendunny. They might have Elsinore too. . . ."

"Levi!" all three kits exclaimed.

"He deserves it!" Dunwattle seethed. He recalled every foul thing that miserable kit had ever done. And how mean Levi had been to Yrynn. But the owls paid no attention to this outburst and continued to explain the threat that New Eden could deliver to the entire animal kingdom. This of course exceeded anything a nasty, snotty beaver kit could do.

"And they might have the swan egg from Belle d'Eau?" Locksley asked.

"Possibly." Flint seemed to growl rather than hoot.

"And our mission?" Yrynn asked.

"To infiltrate the place and gnaw," Delya said.

"No creature can gnaw as you do," Scanda said. "Your teeth and your jaws are as strong as, even stronger than, our wings. You are still just kits. But you are powerful. So powerful." The words reverberated through the air. But the kits didn't feel powerful at all.

"But what are we to gnaw?" Dunwattle asked.

Now Scanda seemed to ruffle up with excitement. "The power cable that the whole of New Eden depends on for its life. You shall shut this place down under the supervision of Blekka the octopus. She will direct you. She knows this evil place as no other creature. She slithers in and out of it constantly, but she will never leave until every creature in it can be free."

"And now during the nights of No Moon and the Red Sprites is the time," Flint said. "The Red Sprites are her camouflage. Maggs has gone to retrieve Blekka. They will return soon. Just watch the sky."

The thunder was still pounding in the distance and the Red Sprites were still dancing through the night. "There she is!" Benjy the tiny snowy hooted. "There's Blekka in the sky."

"Yes, Benjy dear. Isn't that wonderful! She blends right in with the Red Sprites. She's an artist!" Scanda exclaimed.

And all of a sudden there were eight arms streaming down from a fiery blob that the kits presumed to be Blekka's head. The fire of the sprites shifted and transformed into what appeared to be a waterfall of red-hot embers. The three kits tipped their heads up. And then there was a salty smell in the air and an odd voice. "Gentle . . . gentle . . . dearie . . . yes, I must land softly, though boneless I be."

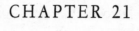

CHAPTER 21

Boneless but Brainy

Dunwattle *looked toward the canopy of the trees through which* something very odd was descending.

"This is the octopus. This is Blekka!" Benjy announced. Yrynn gulped in disbelief.

Blekka's glowing arms like vines descended through the branches of the tree in a slow, undulating air dance. She was a bizarre phenomenon. An extraterrestrial creature, a constellation unto herself, that defied boundaries of land or sea.

Maggs set her down on a slender limb. "Thank you, dear, thank you." The voice issued from somewhere in the tangle of arms. She began to arrange herself by spreading her arms over several branches, and as she did, her intense red color began to fade. As the red dissolved to gray, a silvery glow transformed her into the identical color of the limbs of the rowan tree from which she hung.

"So, these are supposed to be our undercover agents?" She paused. The kits guessed she was looking at them, but it was hard to tell. One eye was much larger than the other.

"Yes, these kits are your agents, Blekka," Flint said. "And kits," the owl confirmed, fixing the young beavers in the glare of his yellow eyes, "Blekka is your spymaster."

"Spymaster?" Dunwattle asked.

"That means she is the director of intelligence in New Eden. She is your boss. She knows everything that goes on there. All the agents take directions from Blekka."

"There are other agents besides us?" Locksley asked.

"Many. There is an orca whale, a great blue whale, and assorted sharks. Half a dozen penguins. But none of the E-Day plans can be executed until you gnaw those cables."

"E-Day?"

"Escape Day," Flint replied solemnly.

Blekka began oozing over a few branches and started to rearrange her arms so she was much closer to the kits. As to whether she was right-side up or upside down, it was difficult to determine.

"Good evening, kits. I am Blekka, but my formal scientific name is Cephalopoda. That is my classification.

This falls under the mollusk order. But you can just call me Blekka."

"Is that what your mom named you?" Dunwattle asked.

"Oh no. When we hatched out . . ." She paused briefly, as if to think. "There might have been twenty thousand of us in the egg clutch, but my mother was dead within days. She would not have had the time nor the energy to name all of us."

"Your mum died when you were just days old?" Locksley asked.

"Yes, dear. That is the way it is for my species."

"Do you just choose to die?" Yrynn asked.

"No, not at all. We do not choose, we just accept."

"It seems unfair," Dunwattle said.

"What is unfair is that animals are imprisoned and made to do the bidding of two-legs! That goes against nature. Our lives and our deaths as ordained by nature are not unfair. It is simply nature. To go against nature is unnatural and vile."

"But you're not allowed to love your children?"

"Allowed to love? Of course, I love my hatchlings. I love them for what they are and what they will become. We octopuses cannot perhaps hold our young'uns and cuddle them in the same way that other animals do, but I swirl and stir water over the eggs and the hatchlings that brings them nutrients. I love them with my eight tentacles that waft those currents over them. I love them with my marvelous brain, and I love them with my three hearts. I am filled with nothing but the most soul-trembling love you could ever imagine. I don't have to be there to love them. I shall love them to the edges of eternity."

Yrynn looked at the creature and thought of her own parents. *Will they love me to the edges of eternity?* She believed they would. This she knew.

Blekka stirred a few of her arms. "But let's move on. I am here to prepare you for New Eden, also known as BIWC. These letters stand for Behavioral Institute for Warrior Creatures." She regarded the confused look in the kits' eyes. "Yes, I know. A bit confusing, but that is the task they have set for themselves at New Eden. Their purpose is to wipe clean the minds of innocent creatures and reinvent them to become weapons of destruction. They do this through hideous drugs and training that numbs their minds."

Blekka's larger eye appeared to fix them in a penetrating gaze. "Your task, or mission, is to infiltrate New Eden and to help us destroy this obscenity. It will be a crucial espionage operation. I am not simply your spymaster, but your asset." *Asset.* The kits had never heard the word. She caught the glimmer of confusion in their eyes with that one weirdly large eye of hers.

"'Asset' is simply the word for the secret or clandestine source inside. But as you can see, I am outside now. Outside because of my peculiar attributes that allow me to slither through just about anything, including the smallest slit, slot, crack, hole, or gap. Of course, I cannot be absent for long or it will be discovered. So, we must act quickly! Let's get started." From beneath her legs, she drew out a coiled piece of paper.

"This is a diagram of the facility. This is New Eden, the most depraved place on earth. Their purpose is to change these animals that they imprison into creatures of destruction—violent destruction."

As the kits studied the map, they were relieved to see there was no indication of any swan's egg. Or any swan, for that matter. And they each vowed not to ask. They were relieved in one sense, but disappointed in another. Their entire mission had been about finding Elsinore, but they certainly had never imagined an egg was part of it. They had a special relationship with Elsinore. Yes, she was First Swan of Glendunny and in that sense a swan for all the beavers in the pond. But she was theirs in another special, inviolable way. A way that was different. They could tell Elsinore things they dared not tell their parents.

Blekka then proceeded to relate the tragedy of Pink the dolphin, who had been fatally injured on a mission to blow up a ship of some sort where good humans worked. The ship from which the good humans worked was an environmental research vessel for the Peacemakers, a group that protected natural resources and endangered species, from plants to animals to oceans and forests. Blekka drew herself closer to the three young beavers and draped three of her arms around them ever so gently. There was a soft little popping sound as the suckers on her arms grasped them. The arms moved just slightly, as if she were tasting them. "Interesting, I've never really tasted fur that much." She paused. "Well, until the otters recently arrived in New Eden."

"You've tasted otters?" Dunwattle said.

"Oh yes, not to eat, mind you. Never! It's just a way of learning about a creature. A family with fur but different from you—another species—was picked up recently by the scouts from New Eden."

"Do you know their names?"

"Of course—Glory is the mum."

"Oh no!" Dunwattle groaned. He knew Glory.

"And her two pups."

"Iggy and Edy?" Dunwattle's voice broke.

"Yes, I'm sorry to say. But they are getting along okay. I taught them how to spit out the capsules."

"What are capsules?" Locksley asked.

"The capsules blue or sometimes green make you slow and dull, dull your brain, and make you forget who you are. Gradually you become their tools—instruments for destruction."

The kits looked at each other. They all remembered

Myrr's description of the night the egg was stolen. The odd discovery of what was floating in the water after they had fallen asleep while guarding the egg, for only a moment. *It was bright blue and about the size of a pebble. It seemed half melted, but there was some sand or white grit in it.*

. "So, you must never swallow any food they give you," Blekka continued.

"But we only eat wood and pond weed."

"Doesn't matter. They will find a way to feed them to you." She spoke in a low, ominous voice and fixed all three with her one enormous eye.

The three kits had never learned so much in such a short time in their lives. Not from their elders back at Glendunny pond. Nor from Mistress Kukla the librarian or Castor Elwyn in hydrology. But they were very glad that Blekka had mentioned nothing about a swan or a swan egg. Nevertheless, they felt compelled to ask her about Elsinore.

Locksley stammered a bit. "By . . . by any chance . . . er . . . uh, can you tell us if there is a swan in New Eden?"

"No, definitely not. If there were, I would know about it."

The beaver kits looked at each other and breathed a sigh of relief.

As for the egg, as far as they were concerned, it was just a rumor told by Luna, a slightly crazy pygmy owl. In their minds, it was absolutely impossible that Elsinore could be connected with that egg. Elsinore didn't need a cygnet, a kit, or anything young to raise. After all, she had them! They were her family, as truly as any young swan could be.

To think that a day before they had never heard the words *infiltration system . . . sterilization procedure . . . pumping stations . . . hydro vacuums . . . electrical grid . . . chem exchange levels . . . reverse hydro expulsion . . .* And now? Well, they felt as if their brains were stuffed with new words and the precise diagrams of New Eden's mechanical systems. All this had to be learned by E-Day. Yes, Escape Day. That was what it had been called. This would be the day that all the mechanical systems would be shut down and the portals and gates and dams of the miles of waterways would open and all the creatures would escape! Nevertheless, they wondered if any of this would get them closer to Elsinore.

But who was it who drilled them again and again on the infiltration plan for New Eden? Who seemed to know the entire layout and design? Who had yet to master flight but knew every nook and cranny of this evil place? None other than Benjy, that tiny snowy owl!

They were all in the big hollow in the rowan tree. The hollow comfortably accommodated the three beaver kits, Benjy, a wisp of a thing, as well as Maggs, Flint, Nebby, and Benjy's mum, Scanda. And now it seemed as if these owls were to be their transport into the most miserable place on earth. A twist in their destinies that was totally unintended and never foreseen.

"But how do you know all this, Benjy? Without even flying?" Locksley asked.

Benjy glanced at his mum. "I overcompensate," he said quietly.

"What does that mean?" Dunwattle asked.

"It means I make up for what I don't have." He fluttered his wings ever so slightly.

"You will have flight, Benjy dear," Scanda said, extending her wing to pat him.

"Oh Mum." Benjy wilfed a bit. Yrynn looked at him carefully. She sensed his embarrassment. She felt terribly sorry for him. Ever since Blekka's visit two days before, she had hardly had time to think of anything else except the complicated maps of New Eden.

Yrynn lingered in the large hollow when the others had left, except for Benjy, who was still studying the diagrams.

"Benjy," Yrynn said slowly.

"Oh, you're still here, Yrynn?"

"Yes."

"You should be getting your rest. Just two more days until E-Day."

"We still have that big problem, though," Yrynn replied.

"Oh." Benjy sighed. Chester was the two-leg who was head operator of the entire electrical grid of New Eden.

They had to distract him somehow so that Blekka could get to the control panel. Blekka could do things with her eight arms and their suckers that no other creature on earth could do. The owls were in awe of her. They brought her a fish once and she demonstrated how to remove all the bones, or "fillet" it, and leave only the meat. "Comes from years of removing those blue capsules," she joked.

"Yes, Chester is a problem, Benjy. You'd realize that if you could fly."

"But I can't fly—not yet. So, stop right there, Yrynn. Remember I'm a late bloomer. I have a few developmental issues, as my mum says. Sounds like I have a talon growing out of my ear or something. Every time Mum tries to make me feel better, it seems worse."

"Don't keep blaming your mum," Yrynn snapped.

Benjy blinked with his large amber eyes. "Don't make me cry, Yrynn. I thought you were my friend."

"I am your friend and I think you can fly."

"How can you—you, a beaver—say that? You can't fly, can you?"

"Well, I was flown here by the owls. I've learned a lot as a passenger. And I can think. I can imagine. I can imagine a wind ruffling through those . . . what do you call them?"

"Feathers."

"No, the ones on the edge."

"Plummels." But then there was that annoying little

voice that always cropped up in Benjy's head when he was trying something new. *So now you're taking lessons from a beaver? Asking a beaver to teach an owlet to fly? Oh, that is something! Shut up!* Benjy thought.

"Yes, plummels. I can imagine all that. And you with your wonderful brain can imagine it even better. Imagine flight will be easy for you . . . and . . . and . . . if you could fly . . ." Yrynn's voice trailed off. "If you could fly . . ." She spoke very quietly now.

"What?" Benjy said. His eyes were open wide. Their yellow light seemed to bore into Yrynn.

"Benjy, if you could fly, you could be the distraction for Chester!"

The mocking voice screamed in Benjy's head. *A distraction. So that's all you're good for. I hardly call that flying.* "Get out!" Benjy shouted this time.

"You want me to get out?" Yrynn was stunned. She thought she was making progress with the little fellow.

Benjy collapsed into a little ball of fluff with his talons straight up, scratching the air in utter despair.

"Benjy," Yrynn said sharply, "pull yourself together. This is outrageously kittish—I mean owlish."

"*Chick*, that's the word," Benjy moaned. "I know! I'm behaving like a chick just out of the egg."

"Exactly," Yrynn said.

"I wish I'd never hatched."

"Well, guess what? You did hatch. Would you rather be like one of Blekka's hatchlings and never even meet your mum? To have her die in the first days or hours of your life?"

"I'm sorry. I know you're trying to help. Sorry . . . uh . . ." *How to explain this*, Benjy thought. "Sometimes I get sort of carried away. I mean, I hear this sort of inside voice—an inner bully—inside me!"

"Well, Benjy, just get rid of that inner bully. Tell him to shut up. Now where were we?"

"Distraction. I'm a distraction—for this two-leg Chester."

"Exactly!" Yrynn exclaimed. "And can you imagine if a bird was discovered in New Eden? That is one of the few creatures they don't have. What a distraction you would be!"

Yrynn paused a long time before she spoke again. She watched Benjy carefully. She knew he was reflecting, thinking deeply about all she had just said.

"Benjy, you are very smart. You explained the Red Sprites to us. You understand so much."

"Except flying, I guess."

Yrynn took a deep breath. "Benjy, I know this sounds strange, but sometimes you have to stop thinking in the usual way and try and simply imagine. You must not simply think, you must imagine flight. While I was flown, first by the eagles and then by the owls, I imagined how their wings were carving and sculpting the air, and the winds. And I don't even have wings! Yet I felt it in some deep part of me."

As Benjy listened, he seemed to be in a trance of sorts.

"I can help you," Yrynn said.

"You mean teach me?" Benjy looked at Yrynn in wonder. "But you are a beaver. You are wingless."

"Not my brain. Not my imagination. It has wings. I have felt the riffles of the wind in my whiskers, the force of a stiff breeze against my broad tail. The fur on my belly has been tickled by the rising currents of air and tousled by the winds off the sea. I am powerless on my own, but I can imagine."

"I will too! Teach me, Yrynn. Teach me to fly!"

And so, in the hours before the dawn, a young beaver began to teach a very young owl how to fly. In the big hollow of the rowan tree, Yrynn said, "Angle your tail feathers, Benjy. When you carve your turns . . . that's it . . . that's . . . it! You got it."

"Brilliant!" There was the low, rasping sound, the signature hoot of a snowy owl. It was Scanda.

"Mum!!!" Benjy screeched, and plummeted to the floor of the hollow, then bounced up again. He batted his wings and was once more aloft!

"Benjy, you are doing it! You're flying! Now follow me

to the top of the tree, and take a look at the stars, the sky, and where you can go with your wings."

"Really, Mum? Really?"

"Yes, my dear, my 'little distraction.'" She made an odd sound that Yrynn realized was a chuckle. It sounded as if a small piece of bark were caught in her gullet. But it was actually laughter. "You will be part of the flyte."

"Part of the flyte!" The very word made Benjy's ear slits tingle. He could never have imagined such a moment, such an event, such a . . . *phenomenon*. The word rose luminous in his brain. Yes, this was simply phenomenal.

Within less than an hour, Benjy had mastered branching. And just as a fragment of the new moon scaled the darkness of the falling night, a flyte of owls rose from the rowan tree together.

PART FOUR

E-Day

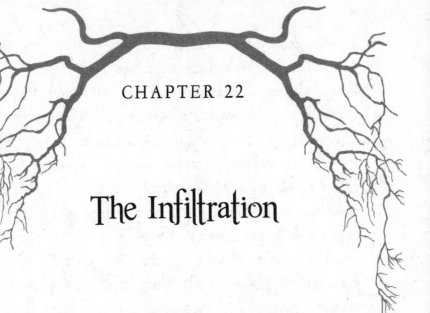

CHAPTER 22

The Infiltration

The flyte was composed of four owls, selected not only for their natural skills but for their feather coloration. It would have to match the dark night mottled with grayish clouds. Most young owlets, after they had mastered branching as Benjy had, flew in the slipstream of their mother or father. The slipstream was basically a partial vacuum from the wake of a bird moving forward through flight. It provided the perfect situation for a young owl in the beginning stages of open flight. However, Benjy could not fly in his mum's slipstream, for Scanda was pure white and would not match the black sky and gray clouds. But Benjy himself was perfect, as his feathers had not yet "turned."

He would be flying in the slipstream of Nebby,

accompanied by three others. Two were great grays who matched the night, and the third was Maggs, the great horned who was considered a "buffer owl." If the operations extended into the dawn, Maggs with her grayish feathers and touches of red and brown could ruffle them to match those hours between dawn and morning. Dunwattle was carried by Maggs, and he wondered what a creature in the early light might think of the great horned with a dark brown blob dangling from its talons.

Locksley himself was preoccupied with the infiltration plan, meticulously reviewing all the details. *No blue capsules. No green capsules. Check all food provided. Cable box—gnaw connecting wires, but not if red light on. Blekka will flip cable box switches, blue light will show . . . blue light good, red light bad . . . blue capsules bad.* How would he keep it all straight? If he chewed a cable when the red light was on, he would be "fried."

Yrynn was hanging from the talons of Flint, and next to Flint was Nebby, in whose slipstream Benjy was flying.

"You're doing great, Benjy," Yrynn said as Flint grasped her tightly.

"Well, it's kinda like cheating, you know. I mean no resistance. I'm in a vacuum."

"Shut up!" Nebby said sharply. "You're not cheating. We'll be dropping you in at dawn minus seven. Now just concentrate on your mission—Chester!!!"

Dawn minus seven was the drop time for the first stage.

The three kits would be dropped near a stream that fed into New Eden. And Benjy would be dropped directly over the complex of New Eden.

Nebby, the wing commander, gave the silence signal with a double wing tip. The first stage of the infiltration would begin with Benjy. They were now flying over the vast complex of New Eden in a lovely thick cloud cover, but Yrynn could see a funneled chimney, called vent 22, rising dimly in the morning mists that perfectly camouflaged the owls. Benjy shot her a quick glance as he dropped out of Flint's slipstream and began carving a turn to fly down vent 22. It was in shutdown mode at this hour of the morning and would deposit the tiny owl close to Chester's control room. "Lovely," she whispered to herself as she saw Benjy tilt his wings perfectly. She felt proud of him. A quiver went through her. She had never in her own short life felt such satisfaction.

Three minutes later, the kits themselves were gently set down on the banks of the stream that flowed out of the Alfamyra River. They soon heard the sputtering sound of a motorboat behind them.

"Just on time." Dunwattle winked at Yrynn and Locksley. It was the sound of the two-leg scouts going out to collect suitable species of animals for their prison. As the boat drew closer, they glimpsed the letters on the side— BIWC. From their coaching with Blekka, they knew what those letters stood for: Behavioral Institute for Warrior Creatures. Then within seconds a net dropped over them.

"Well, what have we here!" a jovial voice boomed.

"Better radio in and tell the Aquarius to set up another freshwater tank."

Aquarius! The word ricocheted through the kits' heads. There could be only one kind of Aquarius in the whole world, and it was a beaver! Not a human two-leg. The title belonged to beavers, and no other leader of an amphibious community, animal or not, could be called an Aquarius. But then the world turned dark as the web of netting dropped over them. Just as planned, they were captured. Their mission was beginning. They were being taken into the heart of all darkness!

And at the same moment that the kits were snagged by the net, Benjy was suddenly sucked down the funnel into the dark world of New Eden himself.

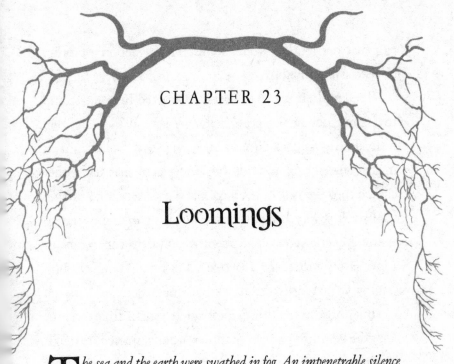

CHAPTER 23

Loomings

The sea and the earth were swathed in fog. An impenetrable silence lay across this nothingness. Elsinore soon realized that all aircraft, including passenger and transport planes, must have been grounded. And she could not be happier. The compass in her brain realigned itself now with the compass in her heart. She knew where she must go—not simply to venture to Belle d'Eau, but beyond—to this strange place called New Eden. She had achieved a high state of vigilance. A state more elevated than schwanka, called *flinck*.

If she had to explain it to another creature, she would say, *It's like building a nest out of the debris of your mind. All the tidbits and scraps come together to form a whole picture.* She recalled her mum telling her this as they built the first nest for the egg that her mother would soon be laying. Soon a brother or sister would hatch.

The muskrat nest had been constructed in a tree stump that stuck out of the pond water by several inches. There were already patches of moss and twigs that had been used in its construction and odd bits and pieces that had either drifted into the nest or been collected by Elsinore to further insulate it. Everything from the shed fur of a muskrat to assorted beetle carcasses, a fragment of a tin can, scraps of a love letter written by a two-leg, and even wild goat dung (highly valued for its insulation qualities).

But those were things one could touch, feel, carry in one's beak. Now, however, other tidbits wafted through her brain, and she flew a few thousand meters above the thick fog.

Then came the shreds of the conversations she had heard between the woman Glencora and her friend Lachlan. There was a moment when Glencora had gasped, "Can you believe it? They've picked up an otter!" And then there was talk about this dark place that was called New Eden. "New Eden," Glencora had repeated slowly. "Now what did you say the longitude-latitude was of this hellish place?"

"It's 62 15.6 degrees north and 006 47.8 west."

"Near that old refueling place we used in the Faroe Islands during the war. We called it Winnie's Pub in honor of Winston Churchill. And now it's called New Eden."

She'd given a rather harsh chuckle. "New Eden," she had whispered. "We could have used that name in one of our spy novels. Clever, isn't it? I hate to think of evil people being clever."

"Look at Hitler," Lachlan had replied bitterly. "Clever monster that one was."

The weight of sadness in the old woman's voice was crushing. All this came back to Elsinore now. She sifted through the words she had overheard while Glencora and Lachlan spoke as they sat listening to Shorty with their earphones. As she recalled fragments—the captured otters . . . the dolphin who died carrying an explosive device . . . a whale . . . an octopus . . . a grand old sea turtle . . . porpoises— a diabolical picture began to form in Elsinore's mind. The "nest" was coming together.

If indeed there was a place—this place called New Eden—where creatures were held captive, could there be an unhatched egg there as well? Humans were always trying to do foolish things like capturing the newly born or in some cases the unborn to be raised in captivity. Thus, the swan began to carve a turn heading south and east as the last piece of this puzzle came to her.

With every mile behind her, with every wing stroke, Elsinore knew she was drawing closer and closer. The egg seemed to call to her. The nest was building in her mind's eye, the twenty-five thousand feathers that had rustled silently in her sleep stirred now around the waking brain that was in a state of high flinck. The egg glowed and beckoned. There was still time. It had been thirty-seven days since she first found the egg. Freshly laid. It would hatch on the thirty-eighth day. She had two days to find it in this diabolical place called New Eden. *I'm coming, chick...* *I'm coming....*

CHAPTER 24

Benjy's Moment

In the half-light of the funnel, Benjy blinked open his eyes. I'm alive, I think. But another voice, that voice that Benjy hated from back at the rowan tree, scraped his ear slits and replied, *Don't count on it.*

I will not be distracted, Benjy thought as he was sucked down the large air filtration funnel. Now where was he? Well, in a funnel. Funnel 4x, in the southeast corner of the complex. The map they had all studied of New Eden was vivid in his mind. He was not that far from Chester in the control room and the switches and dials that controlled the power grid of New Eden. But he must hide until noon, per the plan, which was twenty-six hours from now. Benjy knew about clocks. His great-grandmother had once lived in the clock tower of a church, where she had built her nest. She loved the sound of the chimes that tolled each hour. Unfortunately, the constant tolling had made her deaf, which his grandmother Dorcas considered a blessing. She had grown tired of the long sermons the bishop preached in this place. From Dorcas he learned much about clock time, nothing like creature time, his grandmother explained. Creature time passed with the stars rising and setting and the sky growing brighter in the east and then fading into the glorious colors of the west when the sun set. But in New Eden there was practically no light or windows. Life, if you could call it that, went on in a shadowy world. In addition, there was the constant roar of machinery, air, and water filtration systems. Some of the water seemed to slosh—not like breaking seas, there was just monotonous slapping sounds.

Benjy guessed that the sloshing sounds must be from the watercourses where very large fish swam. And there were pools, not ponds, where the water was still, where the otters and now the beaver Levi were kept. Yes, kept, Benjy thought, in some sort of odd state of suspended life.

Benjy scolded himself. He could not think of that now. He had to figure out where he was. Figure out where the control room was with the man called Chester. He must stay hidden until he could become the best distraction ever.

Then Blekka could slip in and do her work.

And what was her work? Murder.

Far from where Benjy was hiding, Levi gasped as he caught sight of the kits in pool 55.

"What?" Levi's large brown eyes nearly popped out of his head. "What are you doing here?"

"We might ask the same of you," Locksley growled.

Yrynn extended her paw and tapped Locksley's shoulder lightly. "Let bygones be bygones. No time for grudges . . . we have work to do."

"You wanna get out of here?" Dunwattle asked.

"Well, yes, of course," Levi replied.

"You want to help?" Yrynn said.

"Yes, yes!"

"Don't mind mucking around with a Canuck?" Yrynn said. She simply couldn't resist.

"I . . . I never meant anything like that."

"Yes, you did!" she snapped. "But let's get on with the plan. When is the next feeding time?"

"Uh, the last one was just a few minutes ago. Long time until the next one. Hard to tell the time in here. It's like always twilight."

"But there are clocks in here," Yrynn said.

"Oh yeah, those things on the wall?" Levi asked, tipping

his head in the direction of a large clock with iridescent numbers.

"Yes, those things. How many times does the long hand have to go around the clock until it's back where it is?" Yrynn asked.

"A pretty long time, maybe half a day or a night."

"And how many times do they feed you in half a day?"

"Just once."

"Good! In fact, great!"

"Whatever they give you," Levi said in a hushed voice, "whatever you do, do not eat the blue capsules. Never!" he warned.

"We know about the blue capsules or any green ones," Locksley said.

"But we're not going to be eating," Yrynn said. "We are here to gnaw, and you too, Levi. Time to step up and do some real work. Work for the good of all creatures. We are going to gnaw cables. But the most important thing is that we can only gnaw them when the blue light is on, and not the red."

"What happens then?"

"You die. When the blue light is on, the cable boxes have been turned off to check them for something. We don't know what. But they do this several times a day."

"How many cable boxes are there?" Levi asked.

"Only two main ones. We only have to gnaw the main ones."

"Where are they?" Levi asked.

"Between pools fifty-four and fifty-seven," Dunwattle answered.

"The otters are fifty-five," Levi replied.

"Yes," Locksley said. "They can't gnaw like us, but they can be our lookout. And Blekka."

"Blekka! Blekka is nice," Levi replied.

"Yes, and smart. She's our spymaster."

"Spymaster?" Levi asked.

"She plans the operations for E-Day. We—and that means you, Levi—are her agents."

"But there's a two-leg who walks the bridges and checks those cable boxes."

Dunwattle swam up close to Levi. Six months ago, he had loathed this kit. He had wanted to smack him full in the face with his tail. Levi had been a bully, a tyrant to younger kits and especially to Yrynn. But now he felt nothing. Something inside him had grown still. He had no time for hatred, no time for the rivalries of the pond.

"Chester will not walk the bridges or the walkways tomorrow. Because he will be dead."

"Dead?" Levi gasped. "How?"

"Strangulation. Poison."

At that moment, one name flickered in all their minds.

"*Blekka!*" Levi gasped as the realization dawned on him.

Now Dunwattle stepped forward. "There's an orca in here. Hvala, right?"

"Yes, Hvala," another voice answered.

"Who's that?" Dunwattle asked.

"Me!" Glory poked her nose over the adjacent pool.

"Glory!" Dunwattle sighed. "Blekka told us you were here."

"Oh, dear Blekka," Glory murmured.

The other two otter pups poked their noses over the edge. "Is she here?" Edy asked. "She's been gone for so long."

"Yes," Dunwattle replied. "But with good reason. We're getting you out of here. There is a plan."

"What kind of plan?" Levi asked. His eyes narrowed. Dunwattle could almost read his thoughts. *Why are these kits helping me?*

"You mean E-Day is here?" Glory asked.

"It's time." Dunwattle nodded.

And so Dunwattle and Yrynn and Locksley began to explain the escape plan.

"First," Yrynn said, "we need to meet with Hvala because she will be our ride out."

"And then what?" Levi said, still suspicious. It was hard for him to believe that these kits would want to help save him. So Yrynn very calmly began to explain.

"The orca will help us—the beavers and the otters. Since we aren't long-distance saltwater swimmers."

"We are!" Iggy spoke up.

Glory put a paw on her son's shoulder. "Calm down, Iggy. We're no match for an orca."

So Yrynn continued explaining that the orcas, the seals, the walrus, the sea lions—the largest of the sea mammals would be their means of escape.

"And then what?" Glory asked.

"Then comes a flyte," Locksley said.

"A flyte?" Glory asked.

"A flyte of owls and eagles—the eagles of Iolaire. They will transport us to where we want to go—back to Glendunny."

The otter pups looked at their mum. The question was clear in their eyes. *To Glendunny? To the lynx that will devour us?* For wasn't that why they left in the first place? Glory signaled her pups to be quiet.

From the windows in the freshwater pools, they could see a turbulence in the deepwater channel.

"Here comes Hvala," Glory said. The windows filled with black-and-white patchwork. "She's in half sleep," Glory whispered. "It's something whales do. One part of their brain is in charge of sleep. But the other part is awake. It's like sleeping with one eye open."

After a moment, Glory said, "Hvala is stirring now in her half sleep. She knows you're here."

"How?" Yrynn asked.

"She hears you. Orcas have wonderful hearing. She's picked up your . . . your vibrations."

"I'm not vibrating," Dunwattle said.

"Yes, you are!" It was another voice. The eye nearest them in the window blinked.

"Yes, I was expecting you." The orca seemed to sigh, and a series of large bubbles streamed upward. "And when the hour comes, I am your conveyance out of this hell. I am your exit ticket, your evacuation vehicle . . . your *escape!*"

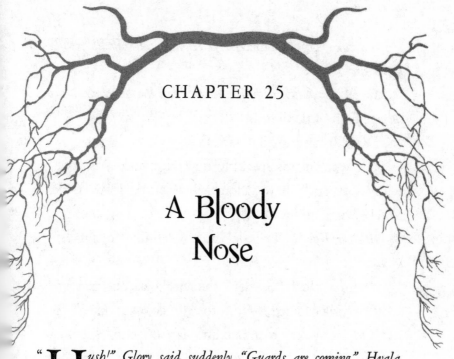

CHAPTER 25

A Bloody Nose

"*Hush!*" *Glory said suddenly.* "*Guards are coming.*" *Hvala* swam on quickly.

"Oh dear," Edy moaned. "It's Red Claws."

"Get over there, Edy, do your thing."

What thing? the kits wondered. They had dived deep, but they watched from a point in the pool from which they could not be seen. As they watched, they saw a slender hand of a two-leg woman sliding into the water. Their eyes opened wide with wonder. They had never seen claws like that—bright red claws! And the claws were picking up Edy and cuddling her. Dunwattle signaled with his own paws in the sign language beavers used when working underwater.

What is she doing to poor Edy? And look at those weird claws.

Not claws, Yrynn signed back. *Humans call them fingernails. But a strange color.*

She could stab Edy with those! I could bite that hand off in two chomps, Dunwattle signed.

Don't! Yrynn paused.

The woman was speaking now. Her voice was gooey with sweetness. "Oh, you adorable little critter. How I'd like to take you home as a pet!"

Bite her! Bite her! Locksley was exclaiming in sign language.

Yrynn stroked Locksley's shoulder with one paw and with her other signed for him to calm down.

"Oh, let me kiss that cute little face of yours," she murmured.

Go for the nose, Dunwattle muttered in sign language.

A shriek suddenly split the air. Blood spurted into the pool, and then a small fleshy thing bobbed on top of the water as Edy was flung back into the pool.

"This cursed animal bit me! Bit me! My nose is half gone. The otter bit off my nose."

There was the thunderous sound of feet pounding down the metallic walkway. "Who's the culprit? Which one! Which otter!" a voice roared.

"The little female."

A long silence followed. "She's . . . she's not here."

"She has to be in there." The muffled words of the

woman came through a bloody towel that she held to her face.

"Just the male and his mother are in there."

"That's impossible."

It would have been impossible if Levi, in an unusual flash of courage, intelligence, and dexterity in the midst of the bloody, churning waters of the otter pool, had not lifted the light little otter from the pool and flung her into his own pool. From there Edy was passed to a neighboring pool and from there to a walrus cave on the rock island in the middle of one of the channels. Blekka in the meantime had passed the alert and mapped out the course. It was ingenious and executed with the highest degree of imagination and collaboration. But the real hero was Levi, who had launched the entire chain of subsequent events after little Edy had clamped down with her very sharp teeth on the two-leg's nose.

CHAPTER 26

The Distraction Goes to Work

All right, all right, Benjy thought to himself. I am in quadrant thirty-five of the complex. So far, so good. No one had spotted the tiny fledgling snowy owl. He had made a perfect landing after being sucked through the funnel. He had angled his wings just as he had been instructed to ensure a soft landing. The drafts in the funnel were not as tumultuous as he had feared. Now his main concern was to keep a low profile as Nebby had instructed. *Well, considering I am too small to have any profile, this won't be hard*, he thought.

But he did have to be alert. When he heard footsteps coming on the walkway, he wilfed. Instantly he grew extremely thin and blended in perfectly with the gray metal grating of the walkway. Had he not moved to the side as a guard walked by, he might have been squashed! *Squashed,* he thought when saw the huge, booted foot of a uniformed two-leg. *What a wretched way to go!*

Squashed was a common cause of death for owls. Usually, they met this fate while flying. Blinded by the headlights of a car or truck, they might slam into the windowpane of a speeding vehicle. That had happened to Dorcas after she had left her nest in the clock tower of the church. She had become unaccustomed to traffic in the small village, and when she got out on the highway, her hearing dulled by the years spent with the chimes in the clock tower, she did not hear the roar of a huge eighteen-wheeler. Benjy's uncle found her an hour later. He swooped down and retrieved her body.

"Glad you got her, Alfie," Scanda had said. "Glad we can have her Finals here. Hate to think of her in some bio lab at New Cavendish University."

New Cavendish University was the last place an owl wanted to end up dead. They had a huge study going on and there was a big wall of drawers especially reserved for owls. The deepest drawers were reserved for the largest owls—great grays, snowies, eagle owls. The shallower ones were for tiny owls like elf owls, pygmies, and so on.

Finally, the sound of the footsteps faded, and Benjy could move on to the next level down, where the control room and Chester would be found. And then it would be showtime!

Yes, "showtime" was what Nebby had called it. "Time to show your stuff, young'un, and be a distraction." It was a wonder to Benjy that five days ago he could hardly fly, but now he had a bag of tricks up his feathers that he could let loose. Aerial somersaults, loop the loops. Zero hour minus two the fun would begin. Benjy and Blekka would converge on Chester in his office.

Everything was going according to plan. Red lights had been switched to blue. The four beavers were in the final stage of their gnawing. Benjy and Blekka would proceed with their tasks. The great whale Hvala swam through the deep channel and rolled a bit to catch a glimpse of Benjy. Hvala gave him a wink as the small owl finished wilfing. *What an amazing creature*, Benjy thought as all thirty feet of the orca slipped past. *She needs to be free! They all need to be free.*

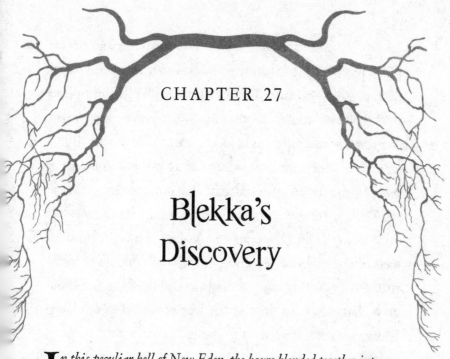

CHAPTER 27

Blekka's Discovery

*I*n this peculiar hell *of New Eden, the hours blended together into one* eternal hellscape. Here animals were drugged and forced through training into unthinkable behaviors that had nothing to do with life. In their greed and hunger for power, the humans were attempting to annihilate any natural instincts a creature might have. Yet the smartest creature in New Eden, Blekka, knew that her own last days were coming as the hour of freedom drew close. Midnight would mean freedom for them all. But hours before the final cables were to be cut, an unforeseen event would occur.

Blekka oozed her way through the various channels and conduits of New Eden. After checking if the red lights or the blue lights were on, she had carefully guided the beaver kits to the essential cable boxes. The gnawing had begun. Blekka left the kits to do their work and now turned to the task at hand—to enter the duct leading to Chester's office in the systems control room. Just as she was about to begin, she spied something high in the rafters. It looked like a strange nest of some sort, made not of twigs and branches but of some other material that did not appear natural at all. The webbing was more closely woven. *What in the world could that be?* Blekka wondered. *Nothing good!* It seemed to reek of malice. And yet through the small openings something within this foul contraption glowed—a luminous glow that suggested life and freedom and maybe even hope. Blekka was determined to find out.

So, the octopus squirmed her way through the maze of the lower duct system to the upper ducts. With her scattered brains, eight arms, and three hearts, Blekka persisted. One heart was circulating the blood, the other two pumping it past her gills to pick up oxygen as she slithered toward the upper realms of New Eden. Her brains were constantly picking up myriads of information.

The air grew warmer and and drier. Nevertheless, the octopus persevered. As she looked down, she saw the four beaver kits diligently turning off the switches in the breaker boxes and then advancing to a nearby junction box, where they would gnaw through the wires. They were naturally intelligent creatures, though not as bright as she was. But they were catching on, she could tell, as to how to temporarily disconnect the electrical grid for brief moments so they could proceed to the major junction, and at that point Blekka herself would press the button in the control room that would open all the portals to the sea and the land outside. By the time their jailers realized what was happening, they would be gone.

The plan was flawless—at least until this moment.

Eggs! The word reverberated through the octopus's scattered brain. She had been trying to ignore that feeling she had had for several days. A dread coursed through her now. Deep within her something quaked in her mantle, which was a muscular cloaklike structure that housed the gills, her three hearts, and many vital organs. There was one part that now bulged with eggs. *Too soon . . . too soon . . . not yet. Not until I am free.* Thousands of eggs that she was incubating and waiting to release when freedom came. But now she saw there was another egg of another creature waiting to hatch. It glowed in the odd nest before Blekka's eyes. She knew it must be a bird egg, for the shell was hard and not jelly like fish eggs. It was large too. But she had no idea what kind of bird. And hadn't she heard Chester musing with the superintendent one recent evening about how they had such a wonderful variety of creatures but were lacking one species—birds! Birds could be vital for their work. "Think!" Chester had said, smacking his lips. "What a large bird and a small bomb—like a grenade could do, Albert! Just think of it!"

With her third arm she touched that bulging sac with her own eggs. But what about this egg before her? Was it to hatch only to become weaponized? What was to be done? Could she save it in any way? She knew that the owls that had delivered Benjy and the beaver kits were waiting nearby for Hvala, their means of escape when the gates to the open sea would swing wide. Could they help somehow and rescue this egg with its unborn chick? *Oh my, this is a distraction*, she thought. *I must not be distracted.* But she felt torn.

A sadness crept into every bit of her tangled body. *Octopuses don't cry*, Blekka told herself. *Never. Crying is for two-legs.* But at this moment she was almost overcome with a need to cry. *Get over it!* a voice seemed to say. *There is work to be done.* She turned away from the nest and began her descent through the network of pipes and vents and channels. If she timed it right, both she and Benjy would arrive in the control room seconds apart. But she was already delayed. Why had no owls mentioned anything about a bird, let alone an egg? They must not have known. After all, she who lived in New Eden hadn't known herself until this very moment.

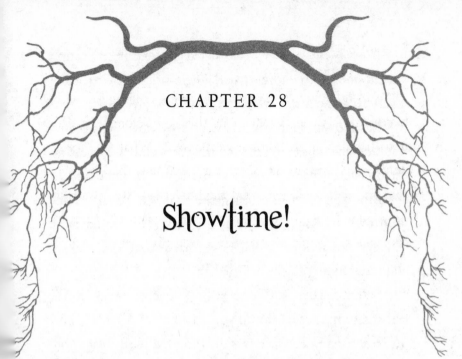

CHAPTER 28

Showtime!

"*I'll catch you, you little devil!*" *Chester had gasped when he first* caught sight of Benjy. He grabbed a flyswatter and began chasing Benjy around the room. It was as if his dream of a bird, a weaponized bird, might come true. Surely this one would grow bigger, big enough to strap a grenade to. But every time he got close, the little bird would dart away. Benjy truly unleashed his acrobatic flying skills—rolls, inside loops, outside loops, tail slides, and lateral skids. Chester was out of breath chasing this feathered devil around his office. He let loose a storm of curse words. At least that was what Benjy thought they were, although he was not familiar with two-legs' bad language. Nevertheless, these words sounded pretty bad.

Where is Blekka? Benjy wondered. He had been putting on the most extraordinary aerial acrobatics act ever. How long could the little owl keep this up?

Blekka was supposed to be here by now. This fellow Chester was chasing him about, but Benjy was getting tired. Then, finally, Benjy saw the tip of Blekka's arm in a ceiling vent over Chester's desk. That was the signal for him to light down on top of the desk! This would draw Chester closer, directly under the "strike zone" for Blekka, who was hiding in the ceiling vent.

"What the devil?" Chester swore at Benjy as he skimmed the top of his head. "How'd you get in here? A bird? A bird in New Eden?" His face was growing red with frustration. It was a fat face, with drooping folds of skin around his jaw.

Blekka could hear the wingbeats as she descended the final meter of the duct that led to the vent. She was fast when she wanted to be. She now slipped the tip of another arm through the vent.

At last! Benjy sighed as he saw the pink tip of the third arm poke through. Her cue! He alighted on top of Chester's computer screen. Exactly where Blekka had told him.

"Well, well . . ." Chester's hand with the flyswatter began to reach out. "What have we here?"

In that same instant, there was a spray of black fluid. Chester began to scream and claw at his own eyes, while

Blekka now dropped through the vent completely and wrapped her eight arms around his neck, leaving him gasping for air. Chester fell back in his chair.

"Is he dead?" Benjy asked.

"No. He'll live. Right now, he is paralyzed by my ink for at least an hour. As I descended through the ventilation system, I decided I would not kill Chester." She paused.

"Whyever not?" asked Benjy.

"I don't want to become like them."

"Them?"

"Two-legs . . . humans." Blekka sighed. "Never!"

High in the pink cirrus clouds that stretched over the dawn sky, a swan spread her wings. Her gizzard quivered with excitement. Excitement and fear. She knew she was drawing closer to that fiendish place where animals were imprisoned and trained to destroy. Where the egg with the cygnet chick was kept waiting to hatch without a mum or dad to keep it warm, to feed it, to teach it to fly. Instead, it would be turned into a devilish tool for two-legs.

Elsinore had no real plan, no strategy on how to rescue this egg. But she would. She was strong. There were myths that swans could break a human's arm. And that was all they were. Simply myths. But they could cause some damage. And if a two-leg came between her and that egg, Elsinore intended to cause a lot of damage. She descended now to a low level and saw the vast complex of New Eden sprawling across the tip of a peninsula. She was almost magnetically drawn to the northeast corner of the complex. She knew, just knew in her gizzard, that the egg was there. She swooped down to a high tower with a half-opened skylight. This was where the egg was! She settled on the edge of the skylight and peered in. The egg glowed.

"I'm here!" she whispered. Then again in Old Swan she murmured, *"Jeg yr gut morun."*

Then, at precisely that moment, a bandaged face appeared and the hand of a woman with bright-red fingernails reached for the egg.

There was a squawk, a scream, and then a crash. Alarm bells screeched. There was a great rushing sound of water as gears began to grind and portals and dikes receded, opening the gates to the sea.

A two-leg was shouting, "We've gone dead! Power out on the master grid. Power out. I repeat, this is a high alert. High alert!!"

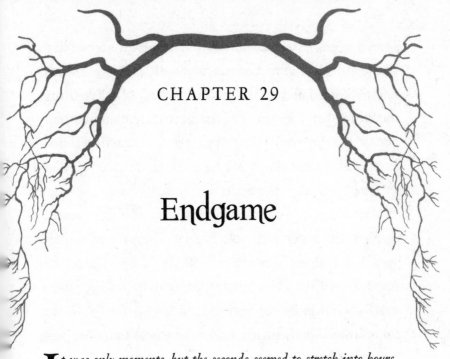

CHAPTER 29

Endgame

It was only moments, but the seconds seemed to stretch into hours. There was the mutilated bandaged face and the red fingernails like deadly talons about to clutch the egg. The egg could be punctured. The cygnet could be stabbed. *I must attack, I must . . .* But then Elsinore envisioned the egg falling, going splat on the concrete floor she had glimpsed below. Could the cygnet survive such a fall? There was no time to think. *Attack and save.* With one foot serving as a cradle with which she tucked the egg into its webbing and using the other as a weapon, she clawed at the woman's head. Blood splattered the air. A scream ripped from the woman's throat. Then, as if blessed by the great swan Cygnus, a convenient warm-air current arrived and Elsinore rose higher and higher, with the egg tucked safely in her lomme, her hidden pocket. The last thing she remembered seeing was the woman half in and half out of the tower window. And yet she had lifted that hand with its red claws, her face bloodied as she raged at the sky, swearing vengeance.

But the egg was warm and safe as Elsinore coasted through the upper thermals. The land below was obliterated. Relief swept through her. She basked in the joy of being away from this abomination of evil two-legs, from this New Eden. But now she was oblivious to all that was transpiring a thousand feet below her where a peculiar procession had begun, from the tip of the peninsula into the nameless bay. Led by an orca, there came a parade of several other whales of various sizes, along with a long line of sea mammals—sea lions, seals, porpoises, dolphins. As well as sharks and sea turtles, ancient and young.

Across Hvala's head, Blekka sprawled with the four beavers and Glory and her two otter pups. The octopus felt weak but happy. Now she must encourage the others. The flyte of birds would soon appear. She would have to bid them farewell, but she must not say a thing about that now. Her intention was to slip away unnoticed. However, now these creatures, on the long back of the gentle orca she had shared so much with, were looking toward her. She knew what they were thinking. Would the catchers from New Eden come after them in their roaring boats, with their horrible nets and dart guns?

Blekka knew that her moment had come. The moment not to die but to lead. She must summon all her strength to encourage these good creatures, these peaceful creatures, these magnificent creatures that blessed the seas of the earth. Grasping with her suckers to Hvala's head, she stretched herself up as tall as a boneless creature could.

"Creatures of salt and sea, wing and gills, fur and claws, creatures of valor. In readiness for this escape, we armed ourselves by resisting the deadening blue capsules embedded in our food. We stayed strong and waited for this very moment. We know that they now chase us with their powerful boats, drop nets, and darts that will numb our brains. But we know one thing . . . we will fight them on the seas, in the air . . . we shall not flag or fail. We shall go on to the end." She tipped her lumpy head toward the sky and saw the flyte coming in. "We shall never surrender!"

As Blekka concluded her speech, it seemed as if a tremor had seized her body, and her skin had grown decidedly pale. She felt as if she had aged years in a matter of seconds, but she still clung to the head of Hvala. And just then the roar of a squadron of powerboats and four helicopters shook the air. She could hear them shouting through the blaring sirens: "Port-side orca . . . ready the darts in the big guns." Blekka thought, *They're going to put us all to sleep. Sleep or sink.* She thought desperately. For those who began to sink in a drugged sleep . . . well, they would sleep forever at the bottom of the sea and never swim again. And those who didn't sink would be hauled in the cast nets and brought back to hell, to New Eden. A thunderous voice now boomed across the whitecaps of the churning water. "Launch Jet Skis to pursue. Load with heavy-duty power-eight tranqs."

"Dive, dive! Dive deep!" bellowed the walrus on the port side of Hvala. Whistling through the air was the sound of the crackle of Tasers and stun guns.

"Deep?" Glory's eyes filled with dark terror. If Hvala went too deep, the otters' and the beavers' heads would be crushed by pressure. They did not have the thick, heavy skulls of whales and sea lions and walruses. But then Glory saw a sleek gray sea lion—she believed his name was Teddy—suddenly go limp in the water. He'd been hit. Not dead, but a boat came by and hauled his body onto the deck. Glory looked about. Around them the sea boiled with explosives and grenades launched from the speeding boats. Blekka grasped Benjy in one of her arms, for he would surely drown when Hvala dived. But what was the choice?

Then suddenly the shadows of wings printed over the tumult of the sea. Owls and eagles darting between the helicopters swooped down. Tracer bullets loaded with tranquilizers sliced through the night. The beavers and the otters felt themselves being peeled from Hvala's back and lifted into the air. The sound of explosives seemed to lessen. Yrynn looked about. They were already high above the sea. *Benjy!* she thought. "Where's Benjy!" she screamed.

A voice croaked from the air, "I have Benjy!" It was Blekka. She was suspended from the talons of an eagle. And cradled in one of her curled arms was the little fledgling snowy owl.

"Is he dead?"

"We don't think so," the eagle said. "But if it hadn't been for this octopus . . ."

"I'm growing weaker. Help me. I can't hang on to him much longer."

In that moment, Scanda slid just beneath the octopus. "Set him down here, on my back, softly. I'll carry him home."

It was a beautiful sight, one Yrynn would never forget. The eagle approached the snowy. In the soft down of Scanda's back feathers, he gently placed the tiny owlet.

"I tried," Benjy said, and looked over at Yrynn. "I tried," he said, looking at Blekka.

"So did I," Blekka said, and dropped into the sea.

That night, Glencora Barrington turned to her old friend as they huddled over Shorty the radio in the barn on Feidah Island. "It's all over," Glencora said, turning to Lachlan MacLean. A look of pure delight spread across her face.

"That it is. They destroyed it. How our old spy unit MI6 got on to it I can't imagine. Shall I pour us a drink to celebrate?" Lachlan beamed.

"I wouldn't turn it down." Glencora lifted the tiny crystal glass that was not much bigger than a thimble. "Skoal!" she murmured, and looked toward the sky. She took a sip and seemed to dissolve into her thoughts.

"I don't think it was all MI6," she murmured.

"A drone?" Lachlan asked.

"Heavens no! Much smarter."

"Then what?"

The old woman picked up a smallish secondary feather, a filoplume. "She left this behind." Lachlan did not have to ask who. They both knew it was the swan's.

"You know what these do, don't you, Lachlan?"

"Yes, sensory receptors. Collect information about wind and air pressure and all that."

"Let's just say she was involved in the end of New Eden.

But I would imagine there were others too."

"Others?"

"Yes, other creatures. I think they might have all banded together. We'll never know who they are." She paused now for a long time. She sighed. "And to think we never knew her name," she whispered as she looked down at the swan feather.

CHAPTER 30

First Crack

T*he egg was indeed a surprise. The kits had tried to will it out of* their minds. But when the rescue owls dropped them back at the pond of Belle d'Eau, there was Elsinore sitting proudly on the muskrat nest. From beneath her they could glimpse the shine of a bluish-gray egg.

"You're staying here in Belle d'Eau?" Dunwattle stared at Elsinore in shock. "I . . . I . . . can't believe it."

"But we just found you," Locksley said. "How can you do this to us?"

The egg was a bit of a shock to the kits. So was the very idea that Elsinore could have any egg, her own or some other swan's, to foster or be fostered by the beavers of Belle d'Eau. But when the owls had dropped them back at Belle d'Eau, there was Elsinore. Elsinore fussing over the muskrat nest with the egg, getting it ready for the moment of hatching.

All three kits were now feeling slightly guilty about their feelings concerning the egg. Yrynn came to her senses a bit before Locksley or Dunwattle.

"It's not like she's doing this to you, Locksley," Yrynn said softly. "This is part of her duty as a swan. She feels she must rescue lost or abandoned eggs. And as she said, every beaver pond deserves a swan."

"But she is doing this to us. And now we don't have one," he protested.

"Yes!" Dunwattle joined in. "Exactly what about us?"

"Stop whining, both of you," Yrynn said in an almost pleading voice. Elsinore gazed softly at her. A dear kit and the most mature, perhaps because she had been an orphan and had to raise herself.

"Kits," Elsinore said, "you are almost grown. But when this egg hatches, this little chick needs to learn about taking care of a pond. How to protect it. How to do flyovers and keep the secret of the beavers in England. You know how important that is. I wouldn't want any of you to wind up as a coat or a hat for two-legs. Even the queen has been known to wear the fur of animals."

There was a tiny sound. "What was that?" Locksley whispered.

"Why, I do believe . . . ," Elsinore said, her eyes opening wide. "I do believe that was the first crack."

"You mean it's coming?" Yrynn almost jumped up and down.

"Slowly," Elsinore cautioned. "It can take a while for a cygnet to hatch. The shell is thick. But see . . . see. That egg tooth."

"Egg tooth?" Yrynn asked.

"Yes, that little bump on the beak that is just poking through. That is what they punch the crack with and make it wider." The beaver kits hunched down close to the nest, resting their chins on the edges.

It was twilight when the first crack appeared. The sky darkened, the new moon rose, then sailed off into another day in another world. The kits stayed through the hours with their eyes locked on the cracking egg. They thought about this new life. They thought about death. They thought about the otter family that one of the eagles of Iolaire was now transporting to Canada on its broad wings. Yrynn couldn't help but wonder when they waved goodbye what that country was like. Might she ever take an eagle to Canada, to her homeland? But in truth she had a deep fondness for Glendunny now.

Another sun rose and set, and the moon began to swell on the horizon. "I think it's close now," Elsinore whispered. The egg had half a dozen cracks and each one was widening.

And then there was one very loud crack and something decidedly unswanlike staggered out from the shell. In the eyes of the kits, it appeared about as attractive as a lump of the mud moss that grew at the roots of cattails. *Ugh!* they all thought. The little chick wobbled to an almost standing position and swung its head.

"Look!" Dunwattle exclaimed. "Its eyes are open."

"Our eyes are never open when we're born, are they?"

"No," Elsinore said. "But swan chicks' eyes are open. Most any other bird or creature's eyes are sealed shut for quite a bit before they open." She turned and looked at the kits. "Do you want to help me now?"

"Help you do what?" Dunwattle asked.

"Help me guide him to the water."

"Him!" Yrynn said. "It's him?"

"Indeed. And after his first swim we should name him."

So, the three kits and Elsinore led the cygnet to the water. The beavers of Belle d'Eau swam around them quietly but at the same time almost burst with excitement. "Our First Swan!" Lily the Aquarius was rapturous. "Now I feel we are here to stay. We have truly a proper pond."

"Look, he's a natural," Locksley exclaimed. And indeed, the little cygnet took right off, staying close to Elsinore's tail feathers while the kits swam behind him.

That night, under the first of the winter moons, the beavers of Belle d'Eau named the cygnet Silvio for his glistening gray feathers that would eventually fledge white. It was not long until Silvio was swimming all around the pond, to the delight of the Belle d'Eau beavers. One morning as they helped Elsinore tuck in some reeds to the nest atop the muskrat's lodge, with the help of Silvio, who was carrying a small twig in his beak, Locksley turned to Elsinore.

"Soon he'll be flying, and then you can come back to Glendunny, right, Elsinore?"

Elsinore shook her head. "No, Locksley."

"No?" Dunwattle and Yrynn both exclaimed.

"Why not?" Dunwattle asked.

"Because that's when his real learning begins. I must teach Silvio the routes." Elsinore sighed. "It will be a while, kits. A year, at least."

"A year!" they all cried at once. This was unthinkable.

"I told you, he has a lot to learn." Elsinore paused here and locked all three of them in her gaze. "And so do you," she said quietly.

"Us?" Locksley said.

"What do we have to learn?" Dunwattle asked. Yrynn remained silent.

"You all must return to Glendunny. I am granting you a *tyllate*."

"What's a tyllate?"

"It's a kind of permission to live in my nest atop the Aquarius's lodge in Glendunny pond."

"But why?" Dunwattle asked.

"You must learn."

"Learn what?" Locksley asked. Hadn't they already learned so much?

It was as if Elsinore were reading Locksley's mind. "You know knowledge comes to one in strange ways."

"What are you saying?" Dunwattle asked.

"I am asking you all to go back to Glendunny. In my nest there is a book—a rather ancient book. With stories older than time—although these are not precisely stories. They are not made up. It is a diary. The diary of Byatta."

"Byatta!" Dunwattle said.

"Yes, Byatta, the First Swan of Great Fosters. The pond of King Henry the Eighth. The swan who led your ancestors, Dunwattle, of the Avalinda line to Glendunny."

"Avalinda!" The three kits seemed to exhale the name rather than actually speak it. This indeed was a hallowed name. For it was Avalinda with the guidance of Byatta who began the secret settlement of Glendunny.

"Before you go forward you must go backward. That is the swan's way of learning. So go back to Glendunny and then back into the history of how the pond came to be. You need to go back a thousand years or more to the time when the beavers of Great Fosters discovered the haunted pond. Only then will you eventually be able to lead the pond."

"Us?" all three kits said at once.

"Us lead the pond?" Dunwattle tilted his head as if Elsinore had just suggested the most impossible and ridiculous thing ever.

But Elsinore continued speaking as if she hadn't even acknowledged their wonder. "You see, kits, it was in fact two cruel kings, Edward Longshanks and Henry the Eighth, who made your existence possible." She paused a long time and fixed the kits in her dark gaze. "Now think about that, young'uns: it was those two savage kings who drove the Great Castor Avalinda to send First Swan of the pond of Great Fosters Byatta on that journey where she discovered Glendunny. Avalinda knew that the end of our species was in sight if King Henry kept killing us for our pelts. And it was Edward Longshanks who laid waste to the village of Glendunny, and that village became a haunted pond perfect for us. Out of evil came good." She now turned toward

Yrynn. "It all began with you, Yrynn. You dared to speak to a ghost."

"Lorna," Yrynn whispered.

"Yes, Lorna," Elsinore replied. "You are a born leader." Then she turned to Dunwattle and Locksley. "You are—all three of you—born leaders."

CHAPTER 31

Life, Death, and Life Again

In the depths of an unknown sea, in the shadows of the roof of her rocky lair, the octopus might appear to be sleeping. Sleeping but much transformed. The tips of her arms hang like pale vines. She is very still except that between the webbing of two arms she appears to hold something. She seems to be guarding what she holds. Her large eye rolls about warily, and then she moves slightly to reveal a thin thread that hangs from the ceiling of the rock ledge. There are actually several threads suspended in the slow-moving currents that stir beneath the ledge. Each has perhaps a thousand or more tiny eggs. She has dedicated these days since her escape from New Eden to the care of these eggs. They are the shape of teardrops. But she is not crying. She is feeling more complete with each glistening strand as she hangs them from the ledge. It's as if she's an artist of creation, weaving a shimmering tapestry—a tapestry of new life.

Some strands are draped around her like strands of a pearl necklace. Beneath this ledge she is shrouded in shadows and completely alone, dedicated to her last task on earth. Protecting the eggs and caring for them is that task. She has stopped eating, because she must dedicate herself to this one endeavor of protecting these strands of teardrops. She grows thinner each day. She strokes them with her suckers and gently blows air and water on them from her gills with the siphon that is tucked beneath her mantle. The babies soon begin to emerge and float away on a current of water, just as the last beats of her three hearts begin to dwindle. And then when her heart stops beating completely, another four thousand have hatched and rain down around her head like a liquid iridescent crown.

Blekka has died. She has died happy. Within seconds of that last beat of her heart, two starfish came and began nibbling on her body. And then a ghost shark came and chased off the starfish. And then Blekka simply vanished.

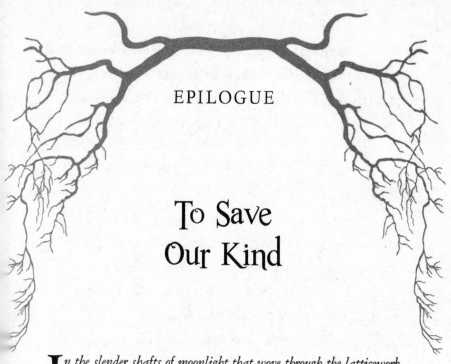

To Save Our Kind

In the slender shafts of moonlight that wove through the latticework of weed and twigs of Elsinore's nest atop the lodge of the Aquarius, Dunwattle opened the ancient tome. On the cover made from the shell of a long-dead spotted turtle, the title had been inscribed in faded letters: **Memoirs of a Swan.** And then beneath it in smaller letters: **Byatta. First Swan of Great Fosters.**

> My name is Byatta. I am First Swan of the Avalinda line of Aquariuses in the pond at Great Fosters during the reign of King Henry the Eighth. In the year of our Lord Great Castor 1540, a little princess wept by the edge of the pond as she saw the newly slaughtered beavers.

"But Elizabeth, my dear . . ." The rather fat king was attempting to console his daughter. "We shall make you a lovely cloak out of this pelt and I shall slay a kit to make you the softest hat with a matching muff. And you shall be very stylish."

"Stylish! I do so want to be stylish, Papa," the little princess said.

And I thought to myself, This has got to end. I must get these beavers out of this foul pond. And so my journey began to seek a place, a very remote place far to the north, where no two-legs would ever come. I went to Avalinda, the Aquarius of the pond, and told her what I had heard.

"Go," she said. "Go now. Before another beaver is murdered, before a kit is murdered."

And so I went. I went and I found Glendunny. To save our kind.